RACHEL L. SCHADE

QUEEN OF STARS AND SPIRITS

A FAE OF BRYTWILDE NOVELLA

RACHEL L. SCHADE

QUEEN OF STARS AND SPIRITS

A FAE OF BRYTWILDE NOVELLA

DRAGON SHADOW
PUBLISHING

MAP OF

WILLOWBARK

ASHWOOD

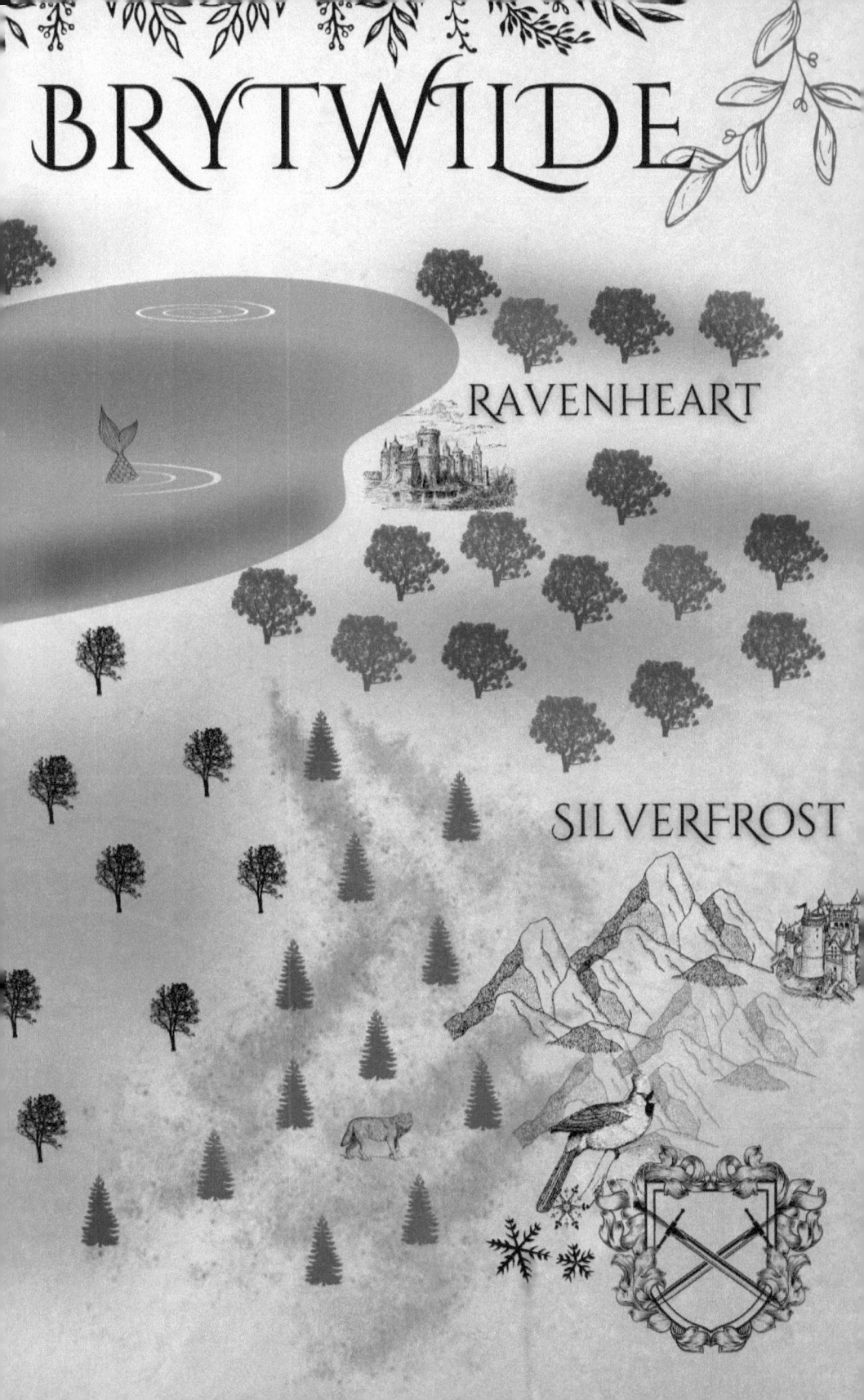

BRYTWILDE

RAVENHEART

SILVERFROST

For the readers who asked me for more.

CHAPTER ONE

C hill air stirred against my face, like an ice-cold finger stroking my cheek or death itself breathing over me. Startled from sleep, I blinked in confusion at the darkness surrounding me. The heavy shadows pooling in the corners of the bedroom told me it was still far too early for Lina or any other servants to be shuffling about, letting in drafts through windows or doors. And Fitz was still asleep—a steady, warm presence beside me. His breathing was rhythmic, his arm still tossed over my waist, holding me against his chest.

But *something* had woken me.

A soft scuffle. Was that movement outside our quarters? Perhaps a restless guard. I nearly closed my eyes again until the whispering started. I strained to pick out words, but unfortunately, the only thing Fitz had shared with me upon our marriage was his elemental magic. Not his keen fae hearing or eyesight, nor his inhuman grace and speed. Not even his ability—and burden—of sending restless spirits on to the peace of the afterlife.

Unease prickled in my chest. What if the whispers were messengers or guards in the hallway, bringing bad news? As the weather grew colder and winter deepened, unpleasant news had become frequent. Ravenheart, the fae summer kingdom and our hostile neighbor, had spurned diplomatic visits and discussions, making us fear what sort of conflict we could be embroiled in once summer arrived. Despite the frigid weather now, summer—when Ravenheart magic would reach its height—felt frighteningly close. Queen Griselda, Fitz, and his brother and sister, Holden and Cordelia, had all been in near-constant meetings this week with their advisors and generals, arguing over whether it was better to play at defense or make an offensive move into the Ravenheart kingdom before summer came. Before we became more vulnerable to whatever they were planning.

I sighed. Perhaps the messengers were hesitating to wake Fitz after a long day, but I knew there was no hiding from the inevitable. Besides, though I'd been holed up with Dahlia more often than not, studying to prepare to become the queen, I'd been permitted to attend a few of the meetings as part of my training. Queen Griselda didn't oblige me whenever I tried to interject my own opinions, saying I wasn't yet knowledgeable enough in the ways of warfare, but at least I was begrudgingly earning a place among the Ashwoods. My people were slowly starting to accept me—or at least, show me respect out of their fear of my powerful husband.

If I asked the guards what gossip they were sharing, they wouldn't withhold news from me. Not anymore.

Regretfully, I extricated myself from my husband's embrace, leaving the warmth of the bed behind and groping in the darkness for my dressing robe. I found it where I'd tossed it haphazardly over an armchair by the fire so I could make myself presentable when Lina wheeled breakfast in. Turning, I nearly stumbled over my discarded dress and boots.

Warmth swept over my skin at the memory of last night's heated kisses, sweet caresses, and whispered words of love. With so few moments with Fitz this past week, we'd made the most of the time we had as soon as we'd reached our shared quarters, and my dress strewn across the floor was the result. I shook my head, trying to dispel the way my chest glowed with joy from what Fitz and I had found. I needed to focus. As my eyes adjusted to the dark, I picked up my boots and stockings and donned them hurriedly.

I cast one last glance over my shoulder at Fitz's sleeping form. Even if I had to return to wake him in a few minutes, it was better to let him rest this short while longer.

Instead, I enveloped myself in my dressing gown, tying the sash and seizing my dagger from my nightstand before strolling through the sitting room and to the front door.

"Ronan?" I whispered when I'd cracked the door. The guard stood stiffly by the wall, his hand resting loosely on his sword hilt.

Brow furrowing, he tossed me a furtive glance. "Do you have a concern, Your Highness?"

I glanced about the hallway, finding nothing but quiet stillness. Silver moonlight bathed paintings along the walls in an otherworldly sheen. "Were you speaking to someone? Whispering out here in the hall woke me up."

Ronan frowned. "I'm the only one posted here tonight, and no one has passed by in quite some time. You must have been dreaming."

A prickle coursed down my spine. Another brush of wind—like a frosty draft—stirred against my cheeks. My hand drifted toward my throat, where Cordelia's locket used to hang. She was no longer a spirit haunting me, but a fae princess brought back to her immortal life and wearing her own magical charm once more. And yet, this all felt eerily familiar. I sucked in a breath.

"Well," I began casually, hoping I wouldn't arouse Ronan's suspicions and provoke some protective instinct that would make him refuse me. "Since I'm already awake, I'm a little hungry. I'll slip down to the kitchen and be right back."

Ronan's throat worked, as if he was considering telling me I would be doing no such thing. But I was no prisoner in Ashwood castle, nor was I an untrustworthy human who'd tricked their crown prince into marriage—not anymore. I was his future queen and under Prince Fitz's protection, now that we'd found ourselves strangely, irresistibly, indelibly in love. My lips twitched briefly at the thought. No wonder Queen Griselda had once asked if I were a witch who'd spelled Fitz. Devotion like ours, especially after our unconventional beginning, was apparently as rare in the immortal world as it was in the mortal one.

"Be careful," Ronan cautioned unnecessarily. Or at least, caution in the castle shouldn't have been needed any longer. Not now that both Prince Fitz and Princess Cordelia—who possessed rare spirit magic alongside the heir to the throne—could send the ghosts on to peace again, there hadn't been any dangers in the castle itself. Instead, the ghosts were secured within the glade of spirits, a place where they could find temporary respite until they were ready, with Fitz's or Cordelia's help, to move on.

But it seemed like something *other* was in the castle tonight, and I knew better than to assume everything was perfectly safe.

Ronan, however, didn't need to know that.

With a cheerful grin, I seized a nearby candle holder, lighting the candle within and stepping past the guard. "I'll return shortly."

As I crept along the hall, my booted steps were muffled by the plush carpet and the flickering candlelight distorted my shadow eerily. I couldn't stop myself from glancing repeatedly to the side, studying the dark figure trailing me, half-convinced it was an apparition. Each time, I silently cursed myself for my foolishness.

Cautiously, I followed the chill breeze licking my face, as if silently urging me toward some unknown destination. Ancient enchantments prevented spirits from entering any of the locked chambers in the castle, but Fitz and I hadn't locked our door for weeks, not since we'd thought he and Cordelia had sent all the ghosts from the premises. But this felt like a spirit. Apparently it was a shy being, not manifesting in our room and not even appearing now, when I was alone in the dark hallway.

"Where are you taking me?" I whispered. "Who are you?"

Help.

The whispered word made my heart jolt painfully against my ribcage.

It didn't make sense. Spirits were drawn to Fitz and Cordelia because of their magic. Since I no longer wore Cordelia's charm, they had no reason to beckon me. I nibbled on my lip as I followed the cold sensation up the stairs and down more halls, winding through the castle until I found myself at the narrow steps leading to Dahlia's library.

"How can I help you?" I searched the shadows for a sign of a spirit.

Perhaps I was being a little reckless and impetuous—again—to follow this ghost alone. But I wasn't the same woman who'd nearly bled out after an encounter with a phouka disguised as my father. Now I was a princess tied to the kingdom of Ashwood and its magic. I might not be able to command souls, but I could fend one off with both my magic and my training.

And I couldn't deny the pull this spirit had on me, the urge I had to help this unseen being, or the way I seemed inevitably drawn up into the library, where the scents of dust and ink wrapped me in their comforting aromas. Everything was as Dahlia had left it after our day of studying. Stacks of books rested in neat piles on her desk and near our armchairs. The cabinet doors that held her teacups and pots were closed. Rows of bookcases bathed in silver starlight, shimmering so brightly through the large window at the far end of the room that I almost didn't need my candle, sat undisturbed.

Further whispering—this time indistinct—made my skin pebble, suddenly making the layers of fabric I wore feel thin and flimsy. The temperature dropped until my breath steamed before me, and I shivered. Wind gusted through the library, puffing out my candle in a stream of smoke.

Stomach churning, I set the holder on the nearest table and slid my dagger from its sheath. Something flashed in my periphery, and I whirled. Nothing.

Turn around, fool, I admonished myself. *Leave. Let Fitz or Cordelia search the library tomorrow. You cannot help a spirit—only they can.*

But if that was true, why hadn't this spirit already revealed itself to them? Why hadn't the return of their magic and the natural order of things compelled this soul to leave and settle in the glade, where it could find peace until it passed into the afterlife?

Teeth chattering, I lifted my chin and scanned the room again. "What do you want?" I asked firmly. "Why did you lead me here?" Hoping to see more clearly and find some solace in my power, I summoned my magic until storm clouds swirled around me, pulsing with electricity that lit up the library with a comfortingly familiar glow. "How can I help you?"

A noise like clothing rustling came from somewhere deeper in the library, among the shelves. I stepped forward warily, keeping my magic close and my grasp on my blade firm. As I drew nearer, the sound of someone weeping drifted toward me.

I peered around a bookcase, glimpsing a crouched form shrouded in shadow.

At my approach, the figure stiffened, its crying ceasing. "Magic," came a hissing snarl, and it vanished.

Faster than I could blink, invisible hands seized my shoulders, bony and strong, slamming me into the shelves. The back of my head smacked against wood. My scalp throbbed and stung. With a muffled cry, I drew my dagger and sliced it through the air, filling the blade with my electricity. It sparked and sizzled. Though I didn't feel myself strike anything solid, the grasp on me vanished.

Spinning for the exit, I dashed from the library. The door groaned on its hinges as I slammed it before hurrying down the steps and into the hall. Darkness pressed on me from all sides—I'd left my now-useless candle behind. Instead, I called on my magic again, letting starlight dance in a swirling cloud of velvet-black darkness by my side, permeating the hallway with a soft, silver radiance.

My head ached, and when I lifted my free hand to my scalp, I found my hair slick with blood. I grimaced. I couldn't shake the sense that an unseen presence continued to trail me through the castle, keeping me on high alert as I searched every corner, every shadow. Keeping my grasp tight on my dagger, I didn't breathe easily until I reached the hallway outside my own quarters.

Ronan tensed as soon as I approached, his expression worried. "What's wrong?" he asked, reaching for his sword.

"Don't be alarmed," I said hurriedly, sheathing my own blade. "I, uh...I was spooked in the darkness."

His eyes narrowed, studying me. "You are unhurt, Your Highness?"

I dismissed my magic, forcing a smile. "Yes, I'm well, thank you. But I think I lost my appetite. I'd rather go to bed." Offering him a sheepish look, I yanked open my door and slipped inside before he could pry me with more questions or notice the blood in my hair.

Softly latching the door, I turned and leaned against it, squeezing my eyes shut. *Why did that ghost want* my *help*? I wondered, thoughts whirling.

A droll voice pierced my churning reverie. "Trying to run away again?"

CHAPTER TWO

F itz paused in the doorway to our bedroom, leaning against the frame. His dark hair was tousled, his loose shirt rumpled, and his bright eyes were alight with mischief. He had no reason to worry, no reason to believe another dangerous ghost might roam the halls or that I'd actually try to flee like I once had, when I'd had no desire to remain married to him. He was only teasing me.

"Not running away," I said, flashing him a grin despite my smarting scalp. "Something woke me."

His eyes dropped to my boots, his brow furrowing. "So you ventured out to wander the castle alone?" He hesitated, blinking. "Do I smell blood?"

Before I could respond, his eyes snagged on my fingers. Blood stained their tips from when I'd touched the back of my head. His gaze sharpened, and a muscle in his jaw jumped. "What happened, Elle?" he demanded, suddenly before me in two long strides. "Who hurt you?"

"I bumped my head," I murmured, reaching to touch the back of it gingerly. "It's not serious, just a shallow cut from one of the bookshelves in Dahlia's library..."

Fitz took my hand and led me into our bedroom, seating me on the bedside while he fetched a bowl of water and a cloth from the washroom. When he returned, a dark threat flared in his eyes. "Do I need to kill anyone?"

I grinned, then hesitated. "He or she is already dead."

In the middle of dabbing at the blood on the back of my head, Fitz stiffened. "How far did you wander, wife?" His tone was careful, measured. He wasn't angry exactly, but I could tell he wasn't pleased. Could I blame him, when my first nighttime venture into the woods had nearly killed me?

Drawing a deep breath, I relayed the pull I'd felt, the chilly draft that had led me to Dahlia's library, and the strange specter waiting within. "It was asking for help, and I couldn't bring myself to ignore it. But why would it linger?" I asked.

Finished with cleaning my injury, Fitz dropped the cloth in the basin and grasped my chin gently in his fingers. "I think the better question is—what did it want with *you?*" His gaze was troubled, his eyes stormy with worry. "You have powerful magic, but not the kind that can dismiss a ghost to the afterlife. I don't want to see you hurt. But I suppose I can't ask you not to wander alone again, can I?"

A guilty smile tugged at my mouth. As if he couldn't resist, Fitz ran his thumb along my lips, tracing my smirk, and I shivered. "No," I breathed against his skin, "I suppose you cannot."

Though concern remained in his eyes, Fitz grinned in response. "Stubborn woman." Sighing, he stepped back, dropping his grasp on me. "At least promise me this: you won't explore that library again at night until you've let Cordelia or me try to communicate with this spirit."

I nodded, despite the doubts twisting through my mind. If Cordelia or Fitz could send this soul to the glade or even the afterlife, wouldn't it have already left? My earlier impression—that this ghost was shy and didn't want to reveal itself to anyone but me—persisted. I just didn't understand what made it think I was the best person to manifest around.

"I'll call for Kinsey," Fitz began, starting for the doorway leading to our sitting room, but I stopped him with a look.

"I'm fine. It's a shallow cut and I didn't hit my head that hard. Could we go back to bed?" My eyes darted to the rumpled sheets, cozy and inviting.

Fitz hesitated, but I stood and sauntered toward him, snaking my arms around his neck and leaning forward until our foreheads touched and our breaths mingled. "Hold me," I whispered. "That's all I need." I didn't add that he looked exhausted and needed the rest. I half-feared he'd call for Kinsey and then leave me with the healer while he ventured off to try to deal with the spirit now. That was the last thing I wanted him to concern himself with after many sleepless nights.

And selfishly, I wanted him to stay with me for a little longer. For nearly a fortnight, I'd been waking in the mornings to find him already gone. I wanted to soak in his presence as long as I could.

I relished the way Fitz's breathing hitched at my nearness, his eyes darkening as they fell to my lips. Pressing a chaste kiss to his mouth, I drew away, lifting an eyebrow as I awaited his response.

My husband's mouth twitched. "I can't say no to you, Blackford."

"A *ghost?*" Grace whispered, her eyes widening as she seized my arm. "Elle, why would you follow one?"

I drew away from her, picking up my pace so I was slightly ahead as we strolled down the hall. The two of us had been summoned to breakfast with Queen Griselda while Fitz and Holden were already ensconced in meetings about Ravenheart. Though I would have much preferred a quiet meal with my mother and sisters than some pompous affair with the queen—who rarely had anything kind to say to anyone in my family—I wasn't upset that the invitation had provided Grace and me with this time alone.

"Think of how Father and Cordelia needed us," I said, folding my arms across my chest. I wasn't chilled, not in the layered emerald gown I wore that seemed far too extravagant for this early in the morning. The urge came from feeling like I needed to hold myself together, like if I clung tightly enough to the hollow pieces of my heart, I wouldn't shatter.

It had only been a couple months since we'd bid Father goodbye permanently. Since I'd been forced to abandon my hope of returning him to the living world. Since I'd had to accept that his loss was irreparable.

Grace quieted. For a few moments, we shuffled on in silence, passing servants who nodded at us politely.

"This spirit seems shy and wouldn't reveal itself until I was alone in the library. And it chose *me*. As if somehow...it wants me to know something or see something." I shrugged helplessly. "I have this feeling that if Fitz and Cordelia couldn't send it off to the glade or afterlife already, if it's been hiding and lurking here while the others have left, that there's something holding it here. And that maybe I'm the only one who can help."

Outside of the queen's private quarters, Grace turned to me, her expression resigned but concerned. "You're capable of many things, so I won't waste time scolding you. I'll only say to be careful, and to *please* listen to Fitz and Cordelia in this matter. Maybe you can help this soul, but that doesn't mean you can send it on to the afterlife. And if its desires regarding you are hostile..." She chewed her bottom lip, clearly thinking of the story I'd shared with her earlier and how the ghost had attacked me. "You're clever. Don't let compassion cloud your judgment."

I stifled a giggle. "My kind-hearted sister telling *me* not to let compassion cloud my judgment? Have we switched places, dear Grace?"

When I nudged her in the side, she burst into laughter. "Perhaps you have begun to influence me."

As the guards swept open the queen's double doors and my sister and I crept into a dimly lit sitting room, we quieted and plastered polite smiles onto our faces. Everything about Queen Griselda's rooms was gaudy and overdone, from the atmospheric lighting she intentionally kept dim with closed drapes and flickering candlelight, to the painted ceilings and countless gilded frames covering nearly every wall. Each individual room was easily the size of Fitz's and my entire suite.

The first room was a grand foyer with a stained-glass-inlaid door separating it from the sitting room. Grace and I shared a hesitant glance before approaching the door, only for it to swing open before we reached it and a harried Dahlia to usher us within. Her short, curvy figure and carefully plaited blonde hair gave her a youthful appearance, but the endless wisdom pooling in her green eyes reminded me she was immortal and had seen more lifetimes than I could even imagine.

"Sit, sit," she urged, closing the door and gesturing toward a settee while she perched in an armchair across from it.

"What are you doing here?" I asked, frowning as I inspected the room and found it void of anyone else, its far door closing us off from the rest of the queen's quarters.

Grace seated herself silently beside me. The only sign of her nerves was the way her knuckles whitened as she carefully folded her hands in her lap.

"Her Majesty wanted me to teach you both a few things and prepare you for your meeting."

I arched a brow at my tutor. "For breakfast? She's had us attend formal feasts with her. What does she expect of us at this private meal?"

Dahlia pressed her lips into a firm line, lowering her voice. "You aren't the only guests. Queen Griselda wanted to welcome some visitors in a smaller setting before any grander announcements are made." Her eyes flitted briefly to Grace before settling once more on me. "There are politics to be considered, and these guests arrived at night."

I frowned. "From another kingdom?" My eyes narrowed. "Ravenheart?" But that seemed too much to hope for, and besides, with tensions the way they were between our kingdoms, there was no way the queen would invite Grace and me to greet Ravenheart diplomats before she scheduled a meeting with the princes.

Dahlia sighed. "Not Ravenheart."

"Silverfrost?" I questioned, though I wasn't sure why they would be here so soon after the recent conflict in their own kingdom.

Flouncing her skirts, Dahlia sighed. "Relationships among most of the kingdoms of Brytwilde are rather tentative, as you know. We are on good trading terms with many of the fae lands across the ocean." She grinned. "Hence why we have delicious chocolates and other luxuries at our disposal." Her expression turned somber again, and she cleared her throat. "But Her Majesty has been in discussions with Willowbark for a while, even before hostilities with Ravenheart became a growing concern. That is where our visitors hail from, and why it's imperative we make a good impression."

My voice turned dry. "She thinks we humans will embarrass her."

"She wants to ensure you're both prepared for a crucial diplomatic visit in a rather unconventional setting. Breakfast may seem casual, but she expects great results."

"Does she think Willowbark will form an alliance to help us fend off the Ravenhearts?" Grace asked quietly.

"If the right conditions are met," Dahlia said, her gaze flicking toward the door. "Be on your best behavior." This comment, I knew without a doubt, was directed toward me. "Let the queen do most of the speaking, but make polite small talk with our guests, Queen Ara and her daughter, Princess Laila."

Before I could open my mouth to ask more, Dahlia rose with a rustle of her skirts and crossed to the door. "Hurry now, before you're late."

As she opened the door, Grace and I stood and crossed toward a vast dining room, where rows of floor-to-ceiling windows granted diners at the long table a backdrop of the wintery forest. Compared to the dim lighting of the other rooms, the golden glow bathing this one made me blink, trying to hastily adjust my eyesight.

At the head of the table, Queen Griselda smiled demurely, looking poised and self-pleased. "How good of you to join us, Princess Elle Blackford. Grace."

Her tone grated on me as I forced myself to dip into a curtsy alongside my sister. I trailed her toward the chairs Queen Griselda indicated on her right, across from two strangers. Princess Cordelia was notably absent, a fact that made me immediately wary. As far as I knew, she wasn't in the meeting with Fitz and Holden this morning either. If this was a diplomatic meeting and the queen's daughter was available, why wasn't she here? Why invite only Grace and me? What was Queen Griselda planning?

I didn't have to wait long for my questions to be answered.

"I'm so eager for you to meet with the good Queen of Willowbark." Queen Griselda's grin broadened. "And of course, dear Princess Laila, Holden's betrothed."

CHAPTER THREE

Every bite of toast was too dry, crumbling like ash in my mouth. My smile was so strained I was certain the Willowbarks could see straight through it to my stewing fury. But for every emotion I was experiencing, I knew Grace's had to be a thousandfold worse.

Whenever I stole a glance at her out of the corner of my eye, trying my best to be discreet, she remained straight-backed and composed. She ate in silence, smiling prettily and speaking only when addressed. Anyone who didn't know her would think she was at the height of peace, content to be invited to a meal with such illustrious company. But I knew her better than that, and I could see the momentary pain flaring in her eyes when she thought no one was looking. I noticed the paleness of her complexion, and the way she nibbled at her food daintily—not out of politeness, but due to a lack of appetite.

How dare you, I thought, grasping my fork in a death grip as I glanced at the head of the table and Fitz's haughty mother. *How dare you arrange this behind my sister's back and then invite her to sit in misery through this farce of a happy morning.*

"Princess?" The hesitant voice made me glance up in surprise, meeting Princess Laila's soft brown gaze. She had smooth ivory skin and an abundance of glossy black hair framing her delicate face. She exuded beauty and innocence in a way that made me hope she had no idea about Queen Griselda's plotting. Yet I still couldn't make myself like her.

I cleared my throat. "I'm sorry, could you repeat your question? I didn't hear you. I was too lost in thought regarding my new mother-in-law's boundless generosity and thoughtfulness."

Queen Griselda took a sip of her tea, her eyes boring into me. I ignored her look, focusing on Laila as she giggled like I'd confessed the sweetest thing. "I was asking about adjusting to life in the fae realm." She twirled her spoon in her teacup as she spoke, her eyes darting between Grace and me as she blushed. "And, well...your husband? Your marriage was also arranged, was it not? I must confess I'm a little nervous, since I hardly know Prince Holden..."

My ears were ringing, nearly blocking out her rambling words. It took everything in me not to rise and shout at the Ashwood queen, not to seize Grace's hand and bolt from the room so she wouldn't have to tolerate another moment of this. I knew the consequences for that would be even worse than what we were being forced to suffer now.

Instead, I grinned in a way I hoped didn't look more like a grimace and took another bite of toast, pretending to muse as I chewed. Laila watched me all the while, patiently sipping her tea and studying me as if her very future hinged on my reply. At last, when I was obliged to accept that Laila's attention wouldn't waver until I answered her, I swallowed. "It's not easy to marry a man you've never met," I said. "I think I speak for every woman when I say we all prefer to bind ourselves to another for love rather than politics."

Laila's smile faltered. Her mother shifted in her seat while Queen Griselda tapped her spoon against the rim of her cup a little too pointedly.

"Of course," I went on, "my family and I are overwhelmed with thankfulness for all the ways in which the Ashwoods have provided for our needs. We want for nothing."

It was a half-hearted kindness, and the princess knew it. While she shifted her focus to her food, trying to pretend that her spirits hadn't deflated at my lack of hopeful words or information about Holden, the queens turned their attention to the finer details of the arrangement. Queen Ara outlined the number of soldiers they were willing to offer, and Queen Griselda haggled her for more until they met at a compromise. My stomach twisted, my appetite fully lost. It was bad enough for this to be happening in front of Grace, but I couldn't help but hurt for Laila too. How awful for one's worth—one's entire future—to be reduced to mere numbers.

"We expect assistance on your end too, as part of the alliance, should the need arise," Queen Ara interjected.

I stole a glance at my sister, who was steadfastly pretending to eat.

Pretending to be perfectly happy. Her eyes were glazed over, as if she were imagining herself anywhere but here.

"What sort of assistance?" Queen Griselda demanded.

"The rest of the kingdoms of Brytwilde are embroiled in conflict amongst one another," the Willowbark queen explained, "but the spring kingdom has been the focus of unpleasant interactions with Emberglade. I will not go into details…but we may need reinforcements from your army."

As our queen nodded, prying her guest for more information about Emberglade and the happenings beyond the ocean that even Dahlia hadn't seemed privy to—not when most of Brytwilde was so consumed with threats from one another—I let their discussion fade into the background. They were troubling matters, but they weren't immediate ones. Ravenheart would raid our castle long before any kingdoms from across the ocean ever set foot on Brytwilde soil. If they chose to at all.

"Grace," I whispered when I was certain Laila was fully focused on the queens' discussion, "are you all right? I could make some excuse about being ill…"

Grace gave me a pointed look. "Elle, you feigned illness a few too many times your first month here. The queen wouldn't excuse us for that now. I'll be fine."

But I noted the way her hand trembled as she set it down in her lap, clenching her napkin in her fist. She was far from fine, and just as blindsided as I had been. Either Holden had known nothing of this engagement, or he'd concealed it from my sister while openly courting her.

"How dare she," I snapped as soon as Grace and I had been dismissed—after the unwelcome announcement that Ashwood was hosting a ball for our guests that very night—and we were safely alone down the hall. "How dare that self-obsessed, abhorrent woman subject you to such humiliation and pain!"

Grace's throat worked as she trailed beside me, her eyes distant, like she was still lost in a haze.

"Did Holden ever speak of this engagement?" I asked.

She shook her head, blonde strands escaping from her careful knot. "But it's not as if..." Grace's voice trailed off as she picked at a loose thread on her sleeve, avoiding my gaze. "It's not as if we had an understanding. He hasn't proposed marriage or anything so permanent, Elle. Perhaps he's grown weary of me, and the pressing needs we have to protect ourselves against Ravenheart made him agree to this arrangement with Willowbark. After all, he and I haven't known one another long, and he hasn't made promises about the future..."

"We might be in the fae world where the rules of relationships and engagements are a little different," I said, "but love looks the same everywhere. I can see it when he looks at you. He *loves* you. I don't think he knows of this betrothal. Ask him! I'm sure his scheming mother arranged this all behind his back. Don't you think it's clear enough from Cordelia's absence? Why would she, a princess by *blood*, not have been invited to that breakfast as well?"

"When she's not in meetings regarding Ravenheart, Cora has been tending to the spirits. That work has kept her considerably busy, since prince Fitz has little time to help her these days." Grace lifted her head, her eyes brimming with tears she could no longer contain.

I wanted to protest, to say that surely for an important diplomatic meal the princess could have taken one short hour away from the work that normally fell to Fitz, but my sister went on.

"What if Queen Griselda didn't arrange this behind Holden's back?" Her voice was raw, tight with a sob she was holding back. "What if he no longer wants me? What if he knows this is his responsibility as prince, and he's glad to be rid of a simple mortal? I'm not like him. I'm shy and awkward. I don't know how to share my feelings. I don't even know if he knows that I—" She choked on her words, lifting a hand to her mouth to stifle the cry that slipped out.

I threw my arms around her, pulling her close as she wept into my shoulder. Shaking, she drew back just enough to finish her confession, her voice soft and tremulous. "I don't think he knows that I love him."

"You need to talk to him," I urged, holding her close. "I'm sure he can clear up all of this."

Grace sniffled as she stepped away. "Even if he doesn't want this be-trothal, he will know it's what's best for his kingdom, and his mother will insist..."

I seized her firmly by the shoulders. "Stop thinking that way, Grace. This is about *your* happiness and *your* future. Don't make excuses and let it slip through your fingers. Fight for it."

Swallowing, my sister met my gaze. "I can try," she said in a small voice.

"You won't have to do it alone," I vowed.

Sweat beaded on my brow as I whirled away from Kinsey's strike, swiftly following the defensive movement with a jab of my own practice blade.

"Well done," he praised when I managed to strike him in the side, successfully ending our match.

Stepping apart to catch our breath, we each scanned the training grounds, where other fae were shooting at targets or squaring off in their own dueling sessions. A handful on the far side of the snowy yard were practicing with magic. A burst of flame permeated the air with the scent of scorched leaves, crisp and sharp—for the crumbling piles lingered eternally beneath layers of frost and snow—before a fae woman calmly guided a stream of water to snuff out the fire.

"Tell me," I said as Kinsey gulped from a canteen and I wiped my brow, "is Holden known to be a rake?"

Kinsey coughed, lowering his canteen to wipe at his mouth and clear his throat. As he collected himself, he studied me with puzzled green eyes. "May I...uh...ask what inspires such a peculiar question?"

I sighed, seizing my own canteen from where I'd rested it on the ground and taking a long pull of water. "I mean, you would warn us if his inten-tions with my sister were anything but pure, wouldn't you? You would tell me if he was toying with Grace's heart. I know you grew up with him, but you're a good man and you've been forthcoming with me. You're my *friend*." I hesitated. "Right?"

Brow furrowing, Kinsey stepped forward. "Of course, Elle. But I'm lost.

Why would you think Holden has been anything but honest with your sister?"

Setting my canteen back on the ground, I swung my practice sword aimlessly through the air. "The queen invited Grace and me to a private breakfast with the Willowbark queen and princess." I struck at a pebble, sending it skittering toward Kinsey's boot. "Queen Griselda announced that Princess Laila is Holden's betrothed, all part of an arrangement to secure an alliance with Willowbark. Did you know anything of this?"

But as soon as I raised my eyes, I could tell this came as a surprise to Kinsey. "If Holden knew anything of this engagement, I'm sure he would have told me." He scrubbed a hand across his face. "He..." Sighing, the fae shook his head, his auburn hair escaping its tie and swishing about his shoulders. "He loves your sister. I've never seen him like this with anyone else. I can promise you that."

Smiling smugly, I nodded. "Good. That's what I thought. Thank you, Kinsey."

Kinsey's eyes took on a faraway look. "So the queen has been scheming all this time. I wonder if she told you before she even informed Holden." His jaw hardened. "When does she plan to announce this publicly?"

"Tonight, at the ball."

"This is..." His words trailed off as he scowled.

"Exactly," I agreed, relieved that someone else was as shocked and infuriated as I was. "We have to stop this. It's madness."

Kinsey sucked in a deep breath. "I agree, but let me warn you in this: Queen Griselda is not easily dissuaded. Not even by her own children."

CHAPTER FOUR

L ina's cheerful humming was a stark contrast to the sleet lashing against the windows. It was a gloomy evening, as dark as my mood.

After breakfast and training with Kinsey, I'd taken time in Dahlia's library to question her about the engagement as well. But she'd been as clueless as Kinsey had. She'd given me a similar warning, reminding me that Queen Griselda wasn't one to *not* have her way, and that the Ravenheart threat would turn advisors and courtiers to her side. Holden's marriage to Grace wouldn't have any political value—not when he didn't need a human wife to help him raise heirs, since that responsibility was expected of Fitz and me.

But I didn't want to think that Holden would be so weak as to give into his mother's domineering ways.

Studying the library's shelves, my eyes lingering on the area where I'd seen the ghostly figure only the night before, I switched topics. "Have you noticed anything strange about the library lately?" I'd broached.

Dahlia arched a brow. "I'm afraid you'll need to be more specific."

"Have you seen any signs of a lingering spirit?"

Her interest piqued, my tutor leaned forward in her armchair, nearly spilling her cup of tea. "Are you saying you have? I thought your husband and his sister have sent all to the glade or into the afterlife."

Cautiously, not wanting Dahlia to fret, I'd relayed the events of last night. "I promise I'm fine," I'd added at the end, when my friend's eyes darted toward my head as if she could assess the damage from several feet away. "It was a shallow cut, and I didn't hit the shelf hard. Not even enough to cause a lasting headache." I paused. "Do you know of anyone who once lived here who was connected to the library as you are?"

"I'm afraid not." Dahlia pursed her lips in thought before standing suddenly, shuffling toward a nearby shelf, pushing a trick button, and revealing a small alcove where a single book rested. With a satisfied smile, she brought back a dusty, leatherbound tome. She set it in my lap, allowing me to scan the book. Both its covers and spine were unmarked, and when I flipped it open, faded lines of differing sets of handwriting filled its pages.

"A journal?" I asked.

"A family journal the Ashwoods of old kept. It's full of royal secrets...but these ones are so old, they aren't exactly confidential anymore. I'd meant to give this to you sooner, to give you a chance to read about the daily lives of past royalty, but..." She shrugged. "Your time in Ashwood has been rather eventful, and I've focused your teachings on more pressing matters, like learning about our relationship with Ravenheart."

"Do you think the ghost has a connection to a member of the royal family?"

Dahlia gave me another shrug. "Perhaps he or she was merely a servant, but this person clearly had a connection to my library. Whether important or not, it's possible one of the past royals shared something that would provide a clue. If nothing else, it's interesting reading material." She winked.

"Do the current Ashwoods know you have this book? Do they keep a journal too?"

She nodded. "Yes and yes. They trust me, and every ruler has kept a journal of sorts like this. After this one was filled, it was stored here in secret, and when the one Queen Griselda—and eventually you and Fitz—write within is also full, it will join this book."

"Thank you."

"I find it interesting that this ghost has only revealed itself to you," Dahlia went on. "Talk to Fitz more—and Cordelia too—and don't do anything dangerous. I know how you like to run off." Her tone took on a scolding note. "But in the meantime, maybe this book could offer some hints as to why this soul wants *you* to be aware of its existence."

Now, watching the sleet pelt my windows, I cast a sidelong glance at the book resting on my nightstand. I hadn't even had a chance to look at it yet. With Fitz, Holden, and Cordelia busy with their tasks and my own schedule filled, I hadn't seen a sign of any of them, either. Just like when I'd first arrived in Ashwood, I couldn't help but seethe with frustration that

Queen Griselda's garish celebrations were cutting into my time.

"You're quiet tonight," Lina observed as she expertly twisted asters and a few crisp autumn leaves, preserved with a spell, into my braid. I watched her with rapt attention in the mirror, amazed that in a few months she'd adapted so well to working with only one hand. She held pins between her lips as she worked, her fingers adept and graceful, able to weave my locks into intricate designs that I couldn't even manage with two hands. When I'd asked her about it before, she'd lightly jested about how her small, unimportant magic had forced her to become innovative in this world even before she'd lost a hand. Now, she had simply learned to be even more creative.

For a moment, I considered opening up to my friend. I'd come to trust her with my secrets, to know she had my best interests at heart and truly wanted to see me flourish in the fae kingdom and my new role as princess. But I didn't want to cause unnecessary fear about ghosts in the castle, or to cast doubt on Fitz's ability to send the spirits on. And the news of Holden's supposed betrothal to Laila didn't feel like mine to share. Besides, speaking the words aloud felt like giving them power, making them real when I was determined that such an announcement would never occur.

Instead, I murmured some excuse about the pressure of learning about being a royal and preparing to eventually rule alongside Fitz.

"There's been gossip about that among the servants," Lina offered after a quiet moment.

Stiffening, I glanced at her expression in the mirror, but she was focused intently on her task of weaving another aster into my hair. "What do you mean?" I asked.

"I mean that they've been speaking about the queen...how she'd had every intention to abdicate soon after Prince Fitz's marriage. But now, with this brewing conflict with Ravenheart, she claims it's best to wait to make the transition."

This was nothing new to me, but I avoided nodding along when Lina was working on my hair.

"The thing is, the people are growing restless. Queen Griselda isn't..." Lina hesitated before lowering her voice. "You're aware of this, of course—but she isn't known for her mercy."

My eyes flicked almost subconsciously to Lina's stump, remembering the awful night when the queen had sliced off her hand.

"Everyone loves you and Prince Fitz. They respect you and your strength, from what you did with securing an alliance with the new Silverfrost queen, to the ways in which you both show mercy and kindness toward the citizens in all your behaviors. Many feel the queen is clinging to the throne out of greed, wanting to keep her power longer than is right. They believe it's time for her to step aside, and they're growing restless."

"No one would risk outright rebellion, would they?" I whispered.

Lina's eyes met mine in the mirror, her expression solemn. "I don't know. But I think they're right. It's *your* time. You and the prince are ready. But I wonder if he hesitates to speak with his mother about it. Maybe if you talked to him and encouraged him..."

My brow furrowed as I considered it. Queen Griselda had held considerable influence over my husband—understandably so—from shaping his mind all his life and grooming him for the throne. He'd adopted her ruthless ways until recently, when I'd helped him start to heal from betrayal within the court when we saved his murdered sister. But just because love had softened him, just because he now esteemed my opinion, didn't erase his connection with his mother. Naturally, he still cared for her, and I couldn't imagine it would be easy for him to pressure her to abdicate.

"I will consider it," I said feebly.

* * *

The ballroom was adorned like a winter wonderland. Everywhere, candles cast a warm, golden glow, and garlands of holly, evergreens, and silver ribbons hung from stairway railings and ceilings. Outside, the sleet had turned into a snowfall that made me grateful for the swiftly burning fires in every hearth in the castle. The ballroom itself was so full of bodies that it was almost stifling. Courtiers chatted, drank fae wine, and casually threatened one another with plastered smiles. But despite the vicious natures of some of our guests, the night's overall spirit was mostly inviting and peaceful. Even the sprites fluttering overhead danced in a way that mimicked the snowfall outside in a mesmerizing display.

"Where's your fierce prince?" The unpleasant voice shattered the momentary peace I'd felt taking in the magical ballroom. I turned to face a courtier whose name I didn't know—one with long, spindly, pale fingers clutching a goblet full of something that looked uncomfortably like blood. His eyes were pupilless, all black and overlarge in his narrow face.

I lifted my chin. "Important meetings have delayed him, but he will be here to welcome our honored guests soon enough."

He took a long, noisy slurp from his goblet, staining his teeth red. His smile was unfriendly—predatory. "I'm surprised how at home you feel, wandering the castle without him."

With a forcibly demure smile, I fluttered my lashes at him. "And I'm surprised you are concerned about my feelings. How thoughtful of you." I flicked a careless hand toward a nearby candelabra, smothering it in the black of night and snuffing out its flames. Smoke curled around us.

Sniffing, the courtier shrugged before forcing himself into a bow and shuffling silently away. I couldn't help the smirk that tugged on my lips as I watched him. I couldn't deny that I relished my new power, the way I could be as fierce and threatening as my new husband. The way I could remind the fae that I wasn't merely protected by Fitz. I protected myself.

As I sauntered through the crowd, determined to show everyone present that I was unafraid, I searched for my family, Queen Griselda, or our Willowbark guests. But I caught sight of Kinsey first, engaged in stiff conversation with a noblewoman that might have been a nymph, her bark-like skin and leafy hair making her stand out even amongst a gathering of creatures known for their otherworldly beauty, horns, and wings.

When I approached, he looked up, green eyes filling with relief, and quickly made his excuses to the woman. Her eyes flashed and her mouth tightened before she bowed begrudgingly and slipped away.

"Not enjoying yourself?" I questioned.

"Making small talk was never one of my strong suits. Your husband and I have that in common," Kinsey confessed, his shoulders lifting sheepishly. "Or perhaps I should say—I despise courtly small talk. The politics, the feigned politeness, the veiled threats. I prefer open and honest communication. If you wish me well, make it plain. If you want to do me harm, draw a sword and duel me. All of these games...it's not to my taste."

I smirked. "What a very un-fae-like confession."

Kinsey's mouth curved in a half-smile. "Perhaps I would fit in more amongst your kind. We healers are generally compassionate—a rare trait for fae folk, I know. Some theorize it is part of the magic we are gifted. We need to care about others in order to wield it."

"Whatever the case, I'm thankful for that. Speaking of compassion and hating trickery...have you had a chance to speak with Holden?"

Kinsey shook his head. "No, and I'm afraid the queen is planning to make her public engagement announcement during some grand entrance with the rest of the royal family." He scowled. "She knows you well enough that she probably hopes to avoid giving you an opportunity to speak to Fitz or Holden before she's already told the entire court."

I curled my hands into fists, my nails biting into my palms. Of course that was what the devious queen had planned. Why had I ever thought I'd have a moment to pull someone aside, a second to gain Fitz's help in stopping his mother, or even a chance to contrive a plan of my own? I wanted to shriek in frustration, to do something wild and impulsive to draw the crowd's attention, but before I could put together some last-minute, hare-brained scheme, the Ashwoods, along with the Willowbark queen and princess, entered the ballroom.

Every head bowed; every conversation ceased. The air seemed to leave the room. Though my eyes darted across Holden's face briefly to try to guess if he knew about the engagement—which, I supposed from his carefree manner, he did not—my gaze didn't linger for long. Instead, I was drawn like a magnet toward my husband. I sought him eagerly, studying his chiseled features and somewhat bored expression as if I hadn't seen him in months.

His bright eyes met mine, that inner flame of adoration reserved only for me visibly sparking. Despite my frustration over tonight, my cheeks flushed immediately in response. The way he could devour me with only a look made my spine tingle. I wanted to pull him in for an embrace and lose myself in his kiss. I wished that we could forget all of this—the politics, the fear, the dangerous courtiers, the queen's schemes—and spend our time in newlywed bliss.

Queen Griselda interrupted my thoughts. "Please show your respect toward our most welcome guests, Queen Nam Ara and Princess Laila Willowbark of the spring kingdom."

I scanned the crowd, heart in my throat, but while I spied my mother and the rest of my younger sisters clustered together near the food tables, munching on fruit and trying to remain inconspicuous around the austere fae, I couldn't see Grace anywhere. Had she managed to excuse herself from the ball? Feign sickness? Lose herself somewhere in the castle halls?

"It is my great pleasure to announce that their visit heralds the start of negotiations for a formal alliance between our lands, beginning with my son Holden's betrothal to the lovely princess." Queen Griselda smiled, but it was all teeth. A dare to countermand her wishes. Though she didn't bother to look in Holden's direction, I knew it was a message for him as well as for Grace and me. It was clear by the shock on his face, which he tried and failed to conceal by lifting a hand to feign clearing his throat. The smile on his lips was forced; his complexion was unusually pale.

I ground my teeth. "That conniving, awful—" I started, thinking of every foul name I'd never dared to utter in my hometown, all too unbecoming for a lady to speak.

Kinsey settled a hand on my shoulder. "Don't react," he murmured. "She wants you to do so in public so the court can see that you're being 'difficult' about the alliance and thus question your future rule."

Swallowing back my disgust, I let Kinsey's logic settle over me. He was right. Of course he was. Queen Griselda had planned all of this, knowing my nature. Knowing how I'd feel and how I'd want to behave. Next to her sons, Kinsey probably knew the queen and her ways better than anyone.

"Thank you," I whispered, straightening and forcing a smile on my face, so the few nobility that had glanced my way—likely curious about my thoughts when they'd seen Holden so publicly with my sister—would only see cooperation from me.

Queen Griselda droned on a while more before ordering the musicians to play and the dancing to start. I took that moment to slip away from Kinsey and approach my husband, who'd already started crossing the ballroom to me.

"A dance?" Fitz asked, arching his brow. Normally, he wasn't comfortable among his courtiers, but now that Cordelia's murderer was dead, he'd become better at being pleasant among his own people. It was easier for him when he wasn't imagining each one as the secret killer of his little sister.

I wanted to protest and lead him away to a quiet corner to discuss his mother's announcement, but then I noticed the look in his eyes. A quiet sort of pleading. *Play along.*

Dipping my head, I allowed him to take me into his arms and sweep me onto the floor. Most of the fae had already started to dance wildly and freely, like they were outside under the stars rather than inside an elegant castle. But Fitz led me in the steps of a more formal dance that reminded me of one I might have enjoyed back home. He kept me close, his warm hands on my hips, his chest pressed against mine.

"You look riveting," Fitz said, dipping his head so his lips brushed against my ear.

Despite the anger still burning through my veins, I shivered at his touch and his words. But I couldn't ignore the question driving me mad. After all, Fitz was the future king. The beloved crown prince that Queen Griselda had carefully prepared all these years to rule. "Holden didn't know of this arrangement," I murmured, pulling back just enough to look up at my husband. With the fae's frenzied dancing and boisterous music, no one but he could hear what I said. "But did *you*?"

I had my answer in his hesitation—the way he swallowed, his throat working. The way he drew a breath before he opened his mouth to respond.

Betrayal stabbed me in the heart. He'd known, and he hadn't stopped it. Hadn't even warned me.

CHAPTER FIVE

"Why didn't you tell me? How could you?"

"Elle—"

Ripping away from him, I fled across the ballroom, ignoring the way I nearly collided with some of the dancing fae as I retreated through the double doors and down the quiet hall. The air was cooler away from the fires and the press of bodies. I crumpled onto the first bench I found, ignoring the guards posted along the walls. Resting my head against the wall, I sucked in an unsteady breath, willing it to dispel my pounding fury and hurt and clear my mind.

Footsteps jolted me from my momentary peace. I couldn't help but toss a scowl toward Fitz as he approached on long strides, his expression unreadable. "Please, I need you to listen to me."

I ground my teeth, voicing my worst fear. "Was it *your* idea?" I demanded.

Fitz's eyes widened in surprise. "Absolutely not. I may see the political advantages, but I don't pride myself in arranging the affairs of others."

"Oh, truly?" I scoffed. "But you went along when your mother proposed it?"

"That is the nature of politics. With the dangers our kingdom is facing—"

"You let her plan behind Holden's and Grace's backs? Helped her keep it secret from them so she could publicly announce it so your brother would be forced into this betrothal?"

This time, frustration deepened his tone as I stood to face him. "Elle, it wasn't like that."

I clenched my fists at my sides, lifting my chin and letting him see the fury flashing in my eyes. He needed to understand the depth of my hurt, the way he had betrayed me. "Then what was it like? Please, enlighten me, dear husband."

Fitz scrubbed a hand through his hair, tousling free the locks that had been tied at the nape of his neck. "You don't understand the sacrifices that must be made. One can never think of his or her own wishes or heart first. Holden and Cora and me? Our futures are dictated by whatever is best for our people. That is all. That is why I agreed to the arranged marriage uniting your family with mine, and why Holden must now agree to this alliance."

Tears stung my eyes. "Grace isn't royal. She shouldn't be asked to make such sacrifices. She's only here because she has nowhere else to go, and she's only had the opportunity to spend time with Holden because *I* took her place. You and I only had the chance to fall in love because I disobeyed your mother's wishes as well! If we'd all blindly obeyed her, then you and my sister would be chained together in a loveless marriage. Now we all have a chance at happiness. How can you not see that?"

Pain filled his eyes, but I turned away. My own vision was blurring with my tears, and I hated that I was dissolving into this weepy mess. "Elle, I never wanted to hurt you, but you *must* see..."

"Then *don't!*" I snapped. "Tell your mother that Holden is promised to Grace. Don't force two people who love each other apart."

Fitz blinked. "I thought she was merely flattered by Holden's attentions."

"She *loves* him!" I bit out. "Just because she's reserved about her emotions doesn't mean she doesn't feel them deeply."

He frowned. "I didn't know."

"Because you never bothered to speak to anyone else about it," I seethed. "You let your mother influence you, just like before. You didn't think about anyone else. Only what she wanted."

Fitz scowled, his emotions clearly oscillating between anger and pain. But I didn't care about his distress, not in that moment. Not when he was the inflictor of such misery on my sister, my dearest friend. The gentlest, kindest person in the world.

He didn't try to deny my accusation as I stalked away, storming back up the stairs. *Curse the ball,* I thought. *Queen Griselda can unleash her anger on me for leaving early. I don't care. She's done enough damage already. She can't possibly hurt us further.*

This time, Fitz didn't follow me.

I couldn't enter our rooms. Not when I knew Fitz might return at any time. I needed space away from him. When I tried knocking on Grace's door, there was no answer. I called out to her, but she didn't respond.

My heart sank. I was sure she was inside her quarters, and it was a low day indeed when she avoided even my company.

"Why weren't you there tonight, Grace?" I called through the door. "You're supposed to fight for your love." My voice broke on that final word, and I rested my forehead against her door, letting a stubborn tear slip down my cheek. Was I a hypocrite for demanding of Grace what I couldn't even do myself? Instead of trying to make amends with Fitz, I'd let anger and hurt consume me.

But how could I possibly forgive him when I knew the depth of pain he was causing my sister?

I glanced out the nearest window at the gathering darkness, enshrouding the winter storm in impenetrable shadows. With the sleet having turned to snowflakes, the steady beat against the windowpanes had melted into silence. All was quiet in this part of the castle, where only a few servants went about preparing rooms for guests or guards stood stoically at their posts.

Weariness sank into my bones, and I longed for rest. There was nothing more I could do tonight for my sister, not if she wouldn't let me in.

Perhaps it was cowardly of me, but I decided to return to my old quarters, the ones I'd stayed in before Fitz and I had fallen in love. I hurried through the halls and then swung open my door. Though I knew the servants kept the quarters clean, even if I hadn't stayed in them for months, the air still smelled stale somehow. The darkness seemed especially heavy, and since no one had lit a fire, an unwelcoming chill permeated the space.

Despite the hollow feeling consuming me, I stubbornly pushed through the sitting room and into my old bedchamber. The bed itself looked vast and vacant. Lonely.

I sighed, but before I could rethink my choice, something struck the side of my face. A shock of pain spread through my cheek as I reached for my throbbing jaw and spun toward the empty corner. A book lay on the floor between it and me—the offending object that had hit me—but my assailant was nowhere to be found.

The cold seemed to deepen, and I realized I could see my breath steaming before me. I failed to repress a shiver as the sensation of icy claws raking down the back of my neck seized me.

The ghost was *here*, in my rooms. Attacking me unseen.

"Who are you?" I demanded.

An angry hiss was my only answer. Something slammed into my old wardrobe, flinging open one of the doors and hurling boots toward me. I ducked and glanced about the room, trying to recall if I'd left anything more dangerous in these quarters.

My stomach wrenched with regret and fear as I glanced back toward my unlocked door. In such a short time, I'd become complacent, assured in my safety, and now it was too late to rectify my mistake. Bile climbed up my throat as a chill wracked my body, the icy breath of the spirit's presence surrounding me.

I tried to focus my tangled emotions, to channel the force of my magic against this malevolent ghost. If I could just use a bolt of lightning, a shock of light, I knew I could frighten the spirit.

Something silver flashed in the darkness, and I stumbled back in alarm. The ghost had seized a dagger from my nightstand. Had I truly forgotten one in here? Or had it found it in some other part of the castle and brought it here? How long had it been waiting and watching me, biding its time for a moment to attack me when I was alone?

My heart pounded as something solid collided with me.

"I'm...not...trying...to hurt you," I grunted, wrestling with my unseen assailant. My hands struck a torso—an arm—the side of a face. Only the dagger was visible as the specter pressed it to my neck.

"You're corrupted," the voice whispered. Icy air rustled against my cheeks, as if the ghost was leaning over me and speaking mere inches from my face. "You use *magic*. You're like *her*."

"Like whom?" I demanded, trying and failing to force the spirit off me. *She's strong for being dead,* I thought wryly.

"Like the one...the one who ruined usss. Curssesss and magic and death. The one who sstole love and life."

The blade dug in a little deeper, nicking my skin. I held still, afraid to keep fighting and inadvertently cut myself more. "A curse to steal love and life? Was it placed on you?"

"On my *family*."

"The Ashwoods?" I demanded.

But the ghost continued her angry rant. "You are like her. Vile. Accursssed. Bloody-handed magical killer!"

That made my fury flare, hot and vicious. This spirit was in *my* rooms, attacking me with *my* dagger, and trying to accuse *me* of being a killer? This time, it was easy to focus my thoughts and emotions, forcing the fearful haze away with my anger. "You're the one trying to hurt me," I snapped, using my fury to fuel my magic. Electricity crackled around us in a stunning violet display.

For a moment, the flare of light shocked the spirit into revealing itself. A young woman, her skin pale as death and blood dripping from her eyes and mouth, hovered over me. Nausea stabbed my stomach as thick droplets of blood splattered against my face, stinging my nose with the stench of copper and death.

I choked on a gag as the spirit vanished, the pressure on me releasing as my dagger dropped to the floor beside me. The overwhelming chill slowly dissipated, and silence hung over the space. Slowly, I sat up and exhaled, finding my face clean of blood. With shaking fingers, I grasped my dagger and hurried to the door to bolt it. I wilted in relief against the door, shutting my eyes and breathing deeply.

A knock made me leap away from my door, muscles tensing as if preparing to ward off another attack, even though I knew ghosts could not pass through locked entrances in the castle.

"Elle?"

It was Cordelia's voice.

I nearly wept from the way the fear deflated from my body as I unlocked the door and swung it open to welcome Fitz's younger sister.

CHAPTER SIX

As soon as she stepped inside, she frowned, scanning me up and down. "Are you hurt?"

I reached up to touch my neck, wondering if the cut was visible. I didn't feel any blood staining my skin. "No."

"Was that spirit troubling you again?"

I swallowed. "Fitz told you about what happened last night?"

She nodded. "And I saw how you two were disagreeing at the ball. You're both quite stubborn and passionate, so I thought I'd find you and see what had happened. When you weren't in your shared rooms...well, I guessed you might come here to your old ones. Can I come in? Did the ghost enter your quarters?" She glanced about worriedly before her gaze settled pointedly on me. "Are you sure you aren't hurt?"

"I'm fine. She's gone now, and I'll be sure to always lock my doors from now on. But I think the ghost truly wants my help. There's a reason she chose me," I insisted. "Even though my magic seems to upset her and make her turn aggressive. I think she might have been a mortal, and that's why she first sought me out. Now she doesn't know if she can trust me."

Cordelia's expression softened into thoughtfulness. "If she really is gone, then come," she said, offering an arm. "Walk with me."

"Did you discover anything else about her? Did she communicate with you?" Cordelia asked as we strolled down the hall. She kept her voice low.

"Not much. She attacked quickly, and then my magic caused her to flee." I relayed our encounter as Cordelia opened the door to her quarters and ushered me into her sitting room. The familiar blue and silver space had once instilled fear, back when Cordelia had haunted them as a spirit. Now, the lingering dust was clean, the rooms cozy and homey, full of dried flowers Cordelia had gathered before winter and the warmth of a crackling fire.

As we settled onto her settee, she declared: "You're right. She's afraid of you."

I raised my eyebrows. "It seems strange to lie in wait for someone you fear."

Cordelia shrugged. "Trust me, ghosts are always afraid, but they're also always trying to find help. She's probably confused, frustrated that someone she thought she could rely on to help her wield magic. She must have had an awful experience with it during her lifetime, or perhaps magic was what killed her."

"If she haunts the library, she may be a member of the Ashwood family. Dahlia let me borrow an old journal belonging to previous royals, but I haven't had a chance to read it yet." I paused, mulling over the spirit's words. "She also mentioned a family curse, one that causes them to suffer and lose love and die." I swallowed. "Could she have been part of the Ashwood family itself? So many troubling things have befallen your family. Your father's death and..." I hesitated.

Cordelia smiled wryly. "You need not tiptoe around the subject of my death. Yes, I was murdered, and that still haunts me, but I am living again. It's not as if your mention of it changes anything." She paused, tapping her chin thoughtfully. "I've never heard of an Ashwood family curse. I always assumed the assassination attempts and my own murder were due to our status, not some curse. And Holden being separated from his love...that's all thanks to my mother's meddling. Maybe the spirit was part of a noble family?"

I frowned. "Maybe." For some reason, that explanation did not feel right, but I also understood Cordelia's reasoning. Though much misfortune had befallen her family, none of it had been particularly mysterious or of a magical origin.

Smiling, Cordelia laid a hand on my arm, stilling me. "As intriguing as this all is, and as much as I want to help you solve this mystery and put this soul at peace, we need to talk about your husband. I know Fitz can be impossibly obstinate..."

"An understatement," I grumbled.

"But he does love you," she finished.

I pursed my lips as if I'd tasted something sour, not wanting to concede her point when I was so upset. "Did you know he was complicit with your mother in arranging the engagement between Holden and Princess Laila?" I hesitated. "Did *you* take part in the planning?"

Cordelia shook her head quickly. "I didn't know Fitz knew about it either. Oh, Elle, I'm sorry." She ran her hands through her blonde locks, which cascaded loosely down her shoulders. "This is why I was so afraid of James and me being caught—before I learned what a monster he was. Mother gets so caught up in her desire to micromanage every aspect of the court in order to best rule her kingdom, she forgets the feelings of her own children. Forgets that *she* once married for love."

"Maybe you could remind her of that? If you side with Holden, perhaps you could plead his case. I can't bear to see Grace's chance of happiness ripped away from her again. It was awful enough when she'd resigned herself for years to her arranged marriage...but when I took her place and she had the freedom to fall for Holden... Cordelia, I haven't ever seen my sister this happy."

Cordelia nodded, her eyes gentle with understanding. "I can try, but I don't think even Holden and I can change Mother's mind. Not when this alliance could save our kingdom if we face a war. She will see it as a way to save lives and show herself as a benevolent, wise queen. Holden's and Grace's love—well, she probably views it as youthful fancy. They are young and haven't known each other long. She didn't even meet our father until she was over a hundred years old. Our handful of decades is nothing compared to the long life she's already lived."

I leaned back against the settee cushions and groaned. "Why must every arrangement involve marriage? In the mortal world, it's a business trans-action. Here, it's a political game. Why can't both kingdoms see they can flourish if they combine their forces? Why do we have to offer your brother to them like he's a pawn?"

Cordelia looked as weary as I felt. "Because the fae kingdoms have a long history of backstabbing one another—sending spies to other king-doms, finding loopholes in alliances and vows and other agreements..." She sighed. "Simple promises aren't viewed as enough when we are all so skilled at weaseling our way out of our own words, even if we can't lie. It's in fae nature—or it's the nature that most of our kind possess, anyway. But a marriage? Willowbark will rest assured that we wouldn't want to cause any harm to their kingdom while Holden is tied to their land, and we would feel confident they wouldn't do anything to us, knowing Princess Laila made her home in our very castle. And even though they're both fae, there is always the hope that their marriage could produce children, another generation that would keep our kingdoms tied together."

"Can't the fae kingdoms find a new way to trust one another that doesn't involve tampering with hearts and futures?" I ground my teeth. "And how could Fitz go along with his mother's scheming?"

Cordelia shot me a look. "He agreed to an arranged marriage. Why wouldn't he expect the same from his brother?"

"Because he sees how happy Grace and Holden are! Because he knows that tearing them apart would devastate them..." I swallowed. "And me." My voice grew smaller. "I cannot bear to see her unhappy."

"You and I know how Grace feels, but she's quiet and shy. My brother is...well, he makes judgments based on what he thinks is logical, and I suppose not seeing her emotions written on her sleeve made him assume Grace wasn't in love. And he figured Holden would be willing to make the sacrifice to save lives." Cordelia bit her lip and fiddled with her skirt. "I'm not sure it can be undone now that the announcement was made to the court and the Willowbark royals are here. Backing out of an alliance is seen as dishonorable. Queen Nam Ara might order a witch to place a curse on our family—or our whole kingdom." She chuckled nervously.

My stomach clenched at the mention of a family curse. I couldn't shake the feeling that what the ghost had said tonight affected the Ashwood royals. Surely in all their generations of rule, they'd offended someone enough. "Are curses placed upon people and families often?"

"Very rarely." Cordelia shuddered. "They are awful things, and the cost required to cast one is great. So great that no witch will agree to placing one for someone else without a large price from the requester as well. But sometimes, the price is believed to be worth it."

I dropped my head in my hands, feeling helpless. "Is there nothing to be done?"

Cordelia rubbed my back soothingly. "I'll try to speak with mother. Try to convince her to talk with the Willowbarks and come up with another way."

Deep down, I knew Cordelia was mostly speaking those words to appease me. Not because she was lying—I didn't believe, even if her fae nature hadn't forbade her to lie, that she had a dishonest bone in her body—but simply because we both knew those efforts were unlikely to provide the results we hoped for.

"Is Grace's happiness to be forever sacrificed for the greater good?" A tear spilled down my cheek, and I swiped it angrily away. "I hate this. I thought I was buying her a chance at something better than the loveless future she always feared, and yet it seems she is doomed to it anyway. And this time it's even worse, because now she's *in* love and knows the pain of heartbreak. If I'd let her marry Fitz, maybe they would have at least become friends."

"And you and he would not be together," Cordelia reminded me gently.

"What do I do?" I asked, lifting my tear-streaked face to study the princess. She was so kind, so gentle—the opposite of everything I'd ever been taught about the fae. In many ways, she reminded me of Grace, and she too had experienced ill fortune in love. Why was it always the gentle souls, the best hearts, who were forced to suffer? To endure heartbreak and sacrifice? What gave me the right to the love I had, and not Grace?

"For now? Read the journal Dahlia found for you. I'll try to speak to the ghost and my mother." Trying to lighten the mood, she winked. "Care to guess which of those situations sounds more terrifying?"

I sniffled through my smile.

"Get some rest. Talk to Fitz. If anyone can convince Mother to change her mind, it will be him."

My heart thudded dully in my ears. "And what if he refuses? I'm not sure I can forgive him for doing this to Grace."

Cordelia reached over to clasp my hand. "I know you can work this out. There's nothing my brother wouldn't do for you, Elle. Believe it."

I wanted to cling to her words, but doubt still squirmed its way through me, muddling my thoughts. Bidding Cordelia goodnight, I trudged out of her rooms and down the hall toward the quarters I shared with Fitz. A strange combination of dread and anticipation rose in my stomach as

I neared our door. Was he still at the ball, or was he waiting for me in our rooms? Would he try to help Grace, or would he insist that she had to forget love for the sake of Ashwood's alliance?

Wiping a weary hand across my brow, I sighed, pausing before I reached for the doorknob. I didn't want to condemn us to a curse or damage the chances we had of an alliance with the spring kingdom. But how could I not think of my sister above others in this scenario? She was the best person I knew, and it wasn't right for Queen Griselda to succeed at her scheming. She knew what she was doing to Grace, and I was certain she was taking a sick sort of pleasure in my sister's hurt.

The door creaked as I opened it, but when I stepped within our rooms, they were empty. Only the quiet crackling of the fire greeted me as I entered our bedroom.

Unsure if I was relieved or disappointed, I picked up the journal Dahlia had loaned to me and sank onto the bed. For a long while, I flipped through the pages without finding anything of interest. The journal entries were full of recordings of political maneuvers, alliances forged and broken, and the constant bickering and battles amongst the fae kingdoms.

But then...I came across an entry in a firm script with the name *Charlotte Berkley, Human Queen of Ashwood* across the top of the first page. Up until then, if any of the other writers had been mortals, no one had revealed it.

My heart pounded in my chest. Even if she didn't share any clues about the spirit haunting the library, maybe this past human queen could share some wisdom from beyond the grave, some pieces of advice I could cling to while navigating this frustrating, dangerous world. Surely the fae of her day had been just as conniving and maddening as Queen Griselda, and just as stubborn and infuriating as Prince Fitz.

I wasn't supposed to marry King Caedmon, wasn't supposed to marry for love at all. I was bound by my word to another, a fae I'd never met.

Back home, Father and Mother always jested that I was cursed with ill fortune. I was clumsy and awkward, struggling to follow the correct dance steps without stepping on toes at town balls. Tripping and losing a slipper in the road when I walked into town. Breaking plates and bumping into furniture.

It seemed harmless enough, if inconvenient, until the day I committed a far worse blunder. I stumbled into a creature of Brytwilde who had wandered into our own town. She was posing as a traveling fortune teller, part of the fall festival to celebrate the harvest and enjoy an evening of merriment and feasting and harmless fun.

When I approached her, I thought I would be asking an elderly human woman to tell me some lies about my future all in good fun.

'Have you come to hear your fortune told by Old Mother Deidre?' she croaked.

'Yes, please,' I said cheerfully, and I let her take my hand in her own, flipping it so she could study my palm.

'Ah, you have great love in your future,' she said with a smirk that revealed yellowed teeth. She went on to describe an idealistic romance with a wealthy and handsome man and a life full of prosperity, health, and happiness. It was exactly the sort of story one wanted to hear when being amused by a fortune teller at a festival, just what I'd expected.

'How shall I pay you?'

Oh, if I could go back and tell myself not to speak to a stranger.

'With a vow.'

I laughed lightly, though a little taken aback. Was this part of the old woman's game? 'What sort of vow?'

'Vow that you will marry the one I told you about.'

'Oh yes,' I said gleefully, sure this was all part of her fun. Who wouldn't want to marry a handsome young man that a fortune teller claimed would bring endless happiness?

That was when I noticed the points of the fortune teller's ears and the gleam in her too-sharp eyes. She was covered in age spots and wrinkles, looking bent-backed and haggard and not at all like the beautiful fae I'd been told stories about.

Terror rooted me to the spot. I should have fled then, should have told her no, but my mouth was full of cotton and my mind wouldn't work. I stared at her, numb. 'You aren't supposed to be here,' I whispered at last.

'Nonsense. I am free to go where I please.'

I swallowed. 'What could you possibly want at a human celebration?'

'I'm growing ancient.' Her smile widened. 'See, I am not like the other immortals, beautiful and forever young. I am a witch...a hag, to be precise...and

it is in my nature to grow ugly. My magic is powerful, but its cost is my youth and beauty. I grow frail, just as other witches and warlocks like me have through the ages. Eventually, my kind choose to pass on to the afterlife rather than continue to wither in this world.

'But I have a son,' she added. 'A handsome, strong, youthful son who will remain strong and handsome all his long days. Before I leave, I want to see him settled with a human wife, one I can expect will bear him children. I want to pass in peace, knowing my line won't end.'

I grimaced. 'Can you not find a fae woman in your land?'

'Bah! The trouble with fae is that our immortality comes with the price of rarely being fertile. It keeps our kind from overpopulating our land until there is no room for us. It forces us to seek out human mates from time to time to increase our odds of bringing children into the world.'

'I see, and I wish you good luck in your search, but I really must be go...'

The witch's hold on my hand didn't loosen as I tried to tug away. 'My son is the one I told you about. The one you have vowed to marry.'

My eyes widened. 'I was playing your game. You spoke of a man of my dreams...some vague idea...' I protested. My mind whirled.

'I spoke of my son,' the hag insisted, her voice growing gruff, her long nails digging painfully into my skin. 'To break your vow to me would be most unwise. I wove a spell over you to bind you to your words. Fail to follow through, and you will die."

The threat in her eyes was real, making my heart pound wildly in my ears. I knew not to question the power of an immortal. I could only imagine what awful death would befall me. 'Give me time,' I said quickly. 'Time to prepare to marry him. Come fetch me at the end of six months' time.'

She scowled. 'Too long. I grow frail. I can give you one week.'

'At least two months,' I pled. I wasn't sure if I would be able to find a way to escape this trap in that time, but it would give me time to say goodbye to my family and friends, if I was doomed to leave this world behind forever.

'A fortnight and not a day more,' the hag proclaimed, finally releasing me.

When I pulled away, droplets of blood glistened on my wrist.

'I will return to collect you then.'

The journal entry ended there. I sat back against the pillows, mulling over what I'd read. Could this human queen be the one haunting the castle? Somehow, she'd avoided marrying the fae she'd accidentally betrothed herself to and had fallen for the Ashwood king instead. Perhaps lingering here in death was part of the punishment she'd brought upon herself for not marrying the witch's son.

"What are you reading?"

I jolted in surprise, lifting my eyes to meet my husband's gaze. He was leaning against the entryway to our bedroom, his expression inscrutable. I'd been so engrossed in the journal that I hadn't heard him enter.

Closing the book, I laid it on the bedcovers. "Dahlia loaned me a journal used by your ancestors in the past."

Fitz gave a single nod.

Silence settled between us. Stifling. Oppressive. I was still angry with him, but I missed him, too. We scarcely had enough time together as it was.

"I thought maybe you would sleep in your own rooms tonight," he admitted at last, not meeting my gaze.

I swallowed. "Is that what you want?"

He lifted his face, studying my expression. "No."

"Then come to bed," I said.

His lips twitched, as if he couldn't decide whether to smile or frown. "No arguments?"

"Not tonight. I'm too tired. In the morning."

Fitz moved about the room quietly as he prepared for bed before settling under the covers on his side. For a long time, we both lay there without speaking, listening to the crackling of the fire and the whistling of the wind through the forest outside our windows.

"Elle..." He began.

"Please don't speak." I rolled over, facing away. "I need time to think."

There was a heavy pause. "Whatever you wish."

I closed my eyes, heart aching. I wished for many things, but my mind was too full. Though I hadn't expected to, I drifted away quickly, swept into a sleep full of dreams about hags with bloodied fingernails and cursed weddings where the bride always ended up with the wrong husband.

CHAPTER SEVEN

Warmth cradled me, and I leaned into it, relishing this beautiful dream. I was with my husband again, with no pain or arguments or betrayal between us. I burrowed deeper into the covers and relished the firmness of Fitz's chest pressed against my back. He sighed, sleepily trailing kisses along my jaw and down my neck.

Desire igniting, I turned to him, wrapping my arms around his neck and tangling my legs with his. His lips found mine, his stubbled jaw brushing against my cheek while his hands drifted to my waist, tugging me firmly against his body. I inhaled, breathing the same air as him as he turned onto his back and pulled me against him. My hair fell around us like a curtain as I leaned forward to kiss him again and again, one hand finding his ear and following its point with my finger. His tongue traced my bottom lip before he bit it gently, and I groaned.

I never wanted to wake from this dream. I wanted to stay here forever, where his warmth felt so real, so comforting. I was surrounded by love I hadn't dared to believe could ever be mine, and I wanted to treasure it always.

One of Fitz's hands drifted lower to caress the curve of my hip before reaching for the hem of my nightdress. He ran calloused fingers beneath the fabric, stroking my thigh.

"Elle." The sound of his voice, raspy and alluring, was enough to wake me fully and make me realize this wasn't a blissful dream. Memories from the night before slammed into me—Fitz admitting to helping his mother plan Holden's engagement to Princess Laila, Grace refusing to answer the door when I went to her rooms. My anger sharpened with my consciousness, stabbing into my chest as I pulled back and rolled off my husband.

"I need to see Grace," I said, sitting up and rubbing my eyes, not even wanting to look at Fitz.

"Blackford." His voice rumbled, reminding me of the way he'd said my name when he'd rescued me in the forest not long after our wedding. A piece of the wall I'd built around my heart cracked, just a little. "Please, let's discuss this. You have to understand I didn't know that Grace cared for Holden so deeply. I thought she appreciated the attention, but not that she was already in love. I knew it would hurt Holden, but he also understands that he has the wellbeing of our kingdom to put first, to ensure lives are protected."

Seated at the edge of the bed, I crossed my arms and squeezed my eyes shut, not wanting to turn to look at him, not wanting to let myself cry. "The problem is that you assumed all that about *my sister* and made that decision without asking her. Or me." I swallowed thickly. "She's my *sister*, Fitz. And you and I are supposed to rule and make decisions for Ashwood *together*."

Silence fell over us like a thick blanket. I wondered if my words had surprised my husband. He was so used to bearing the weight of being the crown prince on his own. He was accustomed to making choices and trusting his own wisdom. To taking on the responsibility for the welfare of his court and kingdom alone.

"It was never my intention to shut you out," he said.

I kept my back to him, lifting my chin stubbornly as I opened my eyes to stand and walk to the wardrobe, selecting a tunic and pair of leggings for the day. "And yet you did."

I fisted the tunic's fabric in my trembling hand, refusing to cry. "I need to go for a walk."

"Don't." Grace's face was pale, dark circles shadowing her eyes, but her voice was unusually sharp as we sat with the rest of our family at the breakfast table later that morning. We, along with our sisters Maggie, Bridget, and Isabel, had met Mother in her quarters for a simple fare of eggs, toast, and bacon. "Don't try to interfere or come up with some scheme, Elle."

I hadn't even spoken a word on the subject yet, but she'd taken one look at the obstinance written across my face and stopped me. I bit my inner lip, longing to argue with her about how deserving she was of happiness, how unfair it was for the Ashwood family to scheme and meddle with her life behind her back.

"It doesn't seem right, though," Isabel murmured, pushing her eggs around her plate.

"Please, Izzy, eat your food like a lady," Mother interjected, sighing in exasperation.

Scowling, Isabel took a careful bite, exaggerating the effort of chewing daintily. Bridget tried and failed to stifle her snort, quickly covering her mouth with her napkin.

"It's true," Maggie spoke up, setting down her book and startling me. I hadn't thought she'd been paying any mind to what was occurring at the table as she'd paged through the tome while nibbling on her toast. "It doesn't seem just or fair that someone else should dictate the outcome of your relationship with Holden and have such sway over your future happiness. The queen made this arrangement without consulting you, even after the prince has spent so much time openly courting you."

Grace sighed, shaking her head and setting down her teacup. "My happiness is of little consequence when this could be a matter of life and death."

It was Isabel's turn to snort. "Will Princess Laila die if she can't marry Holden?" She raised her hand dramatically to her forehead in a mockery of swooning.

"She means the alliance," I volunteered begrudgingly, stabbing a slice of bacon aggressively with my fork. "The fae kingdoms aren't known to get on well unless marriage is involved, and everyone is afraid that without this arrangement, we won't be able to defeat Ravenheart."

"Really?" Bridget raised her eyebrows. "You, Fitz, Holden, and Cordelia are all so powerful in your magic. Those soldiers who fought with..." She cleared her throat, stopping herself from speaking Reid's name when his betrayal of our family was still so recent. "Well, *those* Ravenhearts seemed strong, but you were stronger. Surely our army would be able to fend off anyone who tried to harm Ashwood."

My mind flicked to the memory of the Ravenheart that had held a hand over Reid's chest, drawing out his heart in a gruesome death. But Bridget was right—we had still defeated those soldiers, even with their uncanny abilities. I shrugged. "Apparently, that is not enough to reassure the queen." I took a bite of bacon, chewing it slowly and trying to enjoy the taste despite the emotions swirling in my stomach.

"You should be the queen." Mother's quiet words jolted me from my thoughts, drawing my eyes to her steady, confident gaze. That look—of pride and faith in me—made my heart stir, satisfying an ache I'd long buried within. It was an expression I'd grown accustomed to seeing Father give me, but not my mother. Knowing she believed in me like that was almost enough to temper my foul mood. "You and Fitz have been married for a while now, and it was part of our understanding when we arranged a marriage between our families that he and his wife would take the throne soon after your nuptials."

Isabel smirked. "Perhaps she's still angry that Fitz has the wrong bride." Bridget elbowed her.

"Girls," Mother reprimanded.

I took a sip of tea, relishing the way it settled my stomach. "She's said that this time of unrest isn't when rulership should change."

"She makes excuses," Maggie muttered, picking her book up again and ducking her head back behind its pages.

"Still, your word should hold some weight," Mother pressed on, her gaze steady on me. "Maybe you could discuss this matter with the queen."

I didn't think it was possible for Grace to turn even whiter until she did. "No," she protested. "Don't to that. Don't force Holden into such a position."

I frowned. "What do you mean? Have you spoken to him yet?"

Grace fidgeted with her napkin, throat working. "No, I have not. I don't want to hurt him by making him feel..." She searched for words, shaking her head. "He has the kindest, purest heart. Though he might not be in love with me, he is a dear friend, and I know he would never want to cause me pain. If he had any idea of my true feelings, and what this engagement could do...it wouldn't be right. He knows his responsibility to the kingdom and will want to protect his people. Don't make it harder on him by giving him a reason to hurt."

"Grace, he *loves* you. He's already hurting. There is no way he wants this marriage."

But my sister only licked her lips and shook her head once more.

Sighing, I slumped in my chair. A headache was starting to form, so I massaged my brow absentmindedly as I ruminated over what to do.

Cordelia had already promised to speak to her mother, but the truth of the matter was, Queen Griselda was easily as stubborn as I was.

Which left...what?

I couldn't stand the thought of sitting back and admitting defeat. Perhaps part of that was my own pride, but it was mostly the fear of seeing Grace heartbroken. I didn't want to go against her wishes and speak to Griselda or Holden.

Frustrated, I bid my family goodbye. I passed the day walking through the frosty gardens and then, when I grew too cold and my mind became restless, I went to the library, finding a fae novel to bury myself in.

When darkness began settling over the forest, I once again hesitated at the thought of going to dinner or facing Fitz in my own rooms. Instead, I sought out Grace, hoping she would let me keep her company for a while and maybe take dinner with me in her quarters.

I knocked at her door, hoping against hope she wouldn't ignore me again or turn me away.

This time, she opened her door, her eyes red-rimmed and her cheeks blotchy.

"Oh, Grace." I threw my arms around her neck, squeezing her tightly.

Sniffling, my sister pulled me into her rooms, closing the door behind us. "I don't want to make a scene, so I asked to have dinner in my rooms," she murmured as she led me through the sitting room and into her bedroom, where a four-poster bed and floral coverlets of comfortable down awaited us. We collapsed onto the bed and Grace drew a tray toward us. An assortment of chocolates, fruits, cheeses, honey, jam, and bread were displayed artfully on a platter beside a steaming pot of tea, cream, sugar, and some mugs. "Although, I'm not hungry. But Lina insisted I needed to eat and that these foods provide solace for a broken heart. Especially the chocolate." She smiled at it sadly.

"Well then, we will eat some chocolate and drink some tea, because I'm not going to dinner either." I poured us both mugs, adding cream and sugar to each.

As we chewed our chocolate, relishing how it melted on our tongues, Grace stirred her mug and frowned into her tea.

"You need to talk to him, Grace," I said gently, clasping her hand. "Find out if he knew about his mother's plans. I doubt it. And if not, let your feelings be known. I'm sure he will break off the engagement if he realizes you love him back."

Tears glistened in Grace's eyes. "He's gone," she groaned.

I straightened. "What?"

"The queen sent him away. I finally worked up the courage and went to his quarters to try to speak with him, but the guards posted in the hall told me he'd already left. She sent him away with the Willowbarks immediately after the feast in their honor."

"She sent him away at night? *All* of them?"

Grace studied me helplessly.

"Are you sure the guards weren't twisting the truth somehow?"

Grace shook her head. "They were very explicit in their wording, and when I ran to the stables...I was just in time to see their coach riding through the gates."

Fury ignited in my chest. "Curse the queen. She sent him away to keep him from you. She knows you both love one another, and she couldn't risk the two of you speaking and breaking the engagement she forced upon Holden."

Grace pursed her lips, but she did not argue or try to defend Queen Griselda. Instead, she closed her eyes and leaned back against her pillow with a defeated sigh. "She'll likely arrange for the marriage to take place while he's away, without us in attendance."

If I hadn't been so heartbroken for my sister, I would have grinned with pride at how clearly she saw Griselda's true nature. Instead, I stood and paced. "Then we must find a way for you to go to him."

She frowned. "How? It's not safe to travel through Brytwilde alone as a mortal, and why would I be welcome in Willowbark? Or in their palace?"

"We need an excuse, and we'd send someone to accompany you." I snapped my fingers. "Didn't Lina once mention friends living near the

Willowbark palace? Maybe she could travel with you. That would provide you with company and a safe place to stay, and then you both would have to devise an excuse to visit the palace... But it gives you a chance."

Grace worried her bottom lip between her teeth, seeming doubtful. "Or it could all be for naught. He didn't fight his mother on this. Maybe he wanted to go with Princess Laila. She's beautiful and kind and..."

"You're beautiful and kind. He knows you. He wants to be with you. You just need to let him know how you feel!" I strode toward the door. "Start packing," I tossed over my shoulder. "You and Lina are leaving tonight."

"How?"

"I'm the princess. I'll make it happen."

The air was bitterly cold as I stood in the shadow of the stables, watching Grace, Lina, a coachman, and two guards ride through the courtyard under the cover of night. I'd selected a man and woman I trusted to protect Grace and Lina in their travels, and neither they, the coachman, nor Lina herself had questioned me. I hadn't had much time to discuss everything with them, not wanting to delay and give time for the queen to find out our plans and put a stop to them, but I assumed they were in agreement with me, wanting to see Grace happy as much as I did. Her kindness toward everyone in the castle had made her a fast favorite among the staff.

As the gates groaned shut behind them and the steady beat of horse hooves and creaking wheels trailed out onto the forest path, I breathed a sigh of relief. I'd done it. Now it would be up to Grace and Lina to find a way to speak to Holden, but I was confident if they could, Holden would break off the forced engagement.

I stared into the darkness for a long time, not wanting to return to my quarters and face the tension between Fitz and me, but not wanting to go back to my old ones again, either.

Sighing, I turned, squaring my shoulders as I prepared to face whatever further arguments awaited us until my stubborn husband saw my point of view.

I found myself face-to-face with Queen Griselda.

CHAPTER EIGHT

"Your Majesty." I dipped into a curtsey, keeping my eyes carefully trained on the ground.

"Just as I suspected," Queen Griselda snapped, her lip curling in a most unbecoming sneer. Her raven hair was unbound, hanging loosely down her back in a glossy curtain, reminding me that she was still beautiful and ageless, despite the fact that she had three grown children. She strode closer and glared down her nose at me. "You're scheming." Her eyes flashed, and a chill raked down my back as I remembered the day she'd taken Lina's hand. "You sent your sister after my son so she can try to seduce him and destroy all hopes of an alliance."

Queen Griselda had never liked me, and now I was alone with her.

Even my marriage to Fitz and my future as Ashwood's queen couldn't protect me from her wrath.

"There will be no seducing. He already loves her and you know it." I lifted my chin, refusing to be cowed by her wrath. "Besides, I am surprised at you, Your Majesty. You have such a talent for scheming that I was convinced you would appreciate my own talents."

Queen Griselda's eyes flashed with rage. "How dare you speak so impertinently to me."

"I think you already know that I have dared many things for my family, and I have no qualms about continuing to do so."

She stepped closer, lowering her voice into something that sounded a little calmer, a little more controlled. "You will not interfere with this alliance. Your human sentimentality—your sister's frail little heartbreak—is nothing compared to Ashwood's safety. To Holden's future. I'm not having another son marry into your family. Holden doesn't need heirs, which means I refuse to let him settle for the likes of another lowly mortal."

My blood boiled. "And how dare you decide who your son is allowed to love?"

"Love!" The queen barked out a laugh. "You may think yourself untouchable because of Fitz's attachment to you, but let me make myself clear: you are still nothing but a mortal. The power and influence you wield was gifted to you, and it can be taken as easily as it was shared." She lifted a hand, electricity crackling around her fingers and making the hairs on the back of my neck stand. "And your magic is nothing compared to what we fae can harness."

"Are you threatening me?"

The queen's mouth twisted into an unfriendly smirk. "Foolish, stubborn girl. I am always threatening you. You may have weaseled your way into my family and my son's heart. You may have convinced the court that you belong here. You might even be tied to the land. But you'll never be queen."

"Ah, so you admit the truth." I kept my words even and my back straight, even as I carefully eyed the magic playing around her hand when she stepped closer. "You don't want to relinquish your power. That is the crux of the matter, is it not? You refuse to consider another way to forge this alliance, because you want to be the one in control, the one to save Ashwood from the Ravenheart threat."

Her smirk only widened, a silent acquiescence to my accusation.

"But you are not the one who chooses if I will be queen," I went on. "The land chose me, and I'm as tethered to your kingdom as I am to your son."

"So confident," Griselda scoffed. Her magic flared brighter, spreading out wider. Forked tongues of lightning danced toward me, near enough to threaten but not close enough to touch and harm me. "You forget wives and princesses can be replaced." Clouds formed around us, smothering and dark, curling closer and closer until it felt as if we alone existed in all the world. "You forget the dangers in this kingdom for frail mortal girls." Her eyes flashed with murderous intent as her lightning flared. "You forget it would be my word—the word of Ashwood's immortal, powerful queen—explaining that a horrible accident befell their new princess. Or maybe that you attacked me, and I was forced to defend myself and slay you."

"Fitz would never forgi—"

"You are a silly mortal who stole his magic, his immortality, and his rightful future." Her voice rose. Stormy wind lashed at my face, swirling hair into my eyes. "You think he will choose you? I am his mother. He will always forgive me."

And before I could protest, an earth-rending crashing and splitting tore the air beside me, dulling the rolling thunder. Vines punched through the cobblestones and curled swiftly and tightly about my arms and legs, locking me in place. My eyes widened, my courage withering at this stark reminder that the queen was right about one thing: with my new powers, I had forgotten how vulnerable I still was here. I'd forgotten she was stronger than me, for she possessed the throne and ruled the kingdom. She didn't just wield storm magic like her son. No, she channeled the magic of the autumn land itself in all its forms.

Fear lanced through my chest, as frigid and sharp as one of the icicles clinging to the castle's peaks. I'd mistakenly thought myself untouchable. However ruthless Queen Griselda could be, she loved her children, and I didn't think she'd risk breaking Fitz's heart by killing me. But if she managed to twist her words, to make my death seem like an accident and like the tale she told was true...

My stomach clenched as I tried and failed to summon my own magic. After all I'd overcome, all the risks I'd taken, all the ghosts I'd faced, it seemed especially cruel for my end to come at the hand of my own mother-in-law.

Queen Griselda stepped forward, seizing her chance to unleash her bloodlust upon me while I was trapped and wrapping her long fingers around my throat. I thrashed against her hold, fighting to free myself from the tightening vines. My lungs burned, but my fear was an ice-cold chill encasing my heart.

A gust of wind roared through the thick clouds, parting them into two swirling lines as a dark figure approached through the courtyard. Fitz's eyes blazed with an inner fire, bluer and brighter and more intense than I had ever seen them. His black hair hung in wild disarray about his shoulders as he drew near, lightning crackling at his fingertips. His chiseled features were sharp in the glow of his own magic, etching his face so that it looked as unyielding and unbreakable as stone. His gaze flicked from his mother to the vines twisting tighter and tighter around my limbs, making me squirm in agony.

"You're wrong, Mother," Fitz said, his tone deep and dark and terrible. "I will not forgive you this."

Releasing my neck, she stumbled back as if she'd been struck, her eyes widening with the first hints of fear and doubt. "I am your mother. Your—your queen. I bore you and raised you and taught you... You owe your allegiance to me."

His eyes promised death as he stepped nearer. "Elle is my queen." Thunder reverberated through the air. "I do not care who you are—I will always choose her first. No. One. Touches. My. Wife."

His eyes flared and the air seemed to thicken until I could practically taste electricity on my tongue. The clouds billowed, lightning flashed, and the vines writhed and loosened, compelled by his unseen command.

I gaped, in awe of his power. He'd never commanded nature like this—his magic had always reflected the storms and night skies—but it seemed that the land was bending its will to him, blessing him with greater power. As the heir to the throne, the rightful king, he wielded magic that other fae in Ashwood could only dream of. The vines twisted like snakes and released their hold on me, winding instead with vicious speed toward Queen Griselda. She choked on her startled cry, as if even now refusing to show surprise or weakness, and instead set her face into an expression of stubborn anger as the vines tangled around her own limbs.

She glared at me, as if I had been the one to bind her with the land's magic. "There are consequences for traitors who attack the Ashwood queen," she snarled.

"There are indeed," Fitz cut in. His expression was wrought from steel, the darkness writhing in his eyes the only part that offered a glimpse at the pain he was feeling. "My mother or not, I cannot let this action go unpunished."

This time, Griselda could not conceal her shock and rage. "Elle is not worthy of the title of queen," she spat. "She is a conniving little thief, a trickster who stole your magic."

Fitz shook his head. "She may have tricked me into marrying her, but I shared my magic with my bride willingly. Her or her sister—what difference did it make when all you wanted was for me to marry a mortal? They were both strangers to me. And now the land has seen our bond. It chose her. And your defiance of that puts you at odds with the crown." His tone pitched low. Dangerous. "With me."

Griselda's throat worked as she swallowed. Though the vines pinched at her arms and legs tightly, she kept her head high, her posture proud. "Are you to kill me then, son? To choose her over your own flesh and blood?"

Fitz's voice pitched low. "Never. But don't think this will go without repercussions. You will not lay a hand on my wife ever again. And your treason has cost you your throne and your dignity."

Before Griselda could protest, Fitz called out, summoning guards from their posts on the ramparts. They emerged from the shadows and obeyed their prince without question when he told them to cut Griselda from the vines and restrain her.

"Take her to the dungeons," he went on. "I will deal with her later according to her crimes."

Clinging to the remnants of her pride, a pale Griselda didn't speak or resist the guards, instead stiffly allowing them to lead her away in chains.

Meanwhile, Fitz slipped his arm around my waist and tugged me gently yet firmly from the courtyard, leaving his mother knotted amongst the vegetation like a prisoner.

As soon as we were back in the castle, Fitz turned to me, his gaze sweeping over me from head to toe. "Are you hurt?" He brushed a tendril of hair behind my ear, softening my heart despite our earlier quarrels, and then his thumbs cautiously caressed my throat.

I shook my head. "Not badly." My voice was a little raspy, but it was nothing compared to when Cordelia's spirit had attacked me. "I don't need Kinsey," I added before he could suggest a healer. "Not now anyway. Let's not cause any more fuss just yet."

I knew that, though the kingdom would support their crown prince, they would be less thrilled about me stepping into their queen's role. They would trust his word that Griselda had committed treason, but that didn't mean they would like the consequences or make the transition easy for us.

Fitz was quiet for a long moment, taking my elbow and ushering me up the stairs and down our hallway, past familiar portraits and windows open to the forest, adorned in icicles that glistened silver in the moonlight. "Elle, was this about the alliance?"

"Your mother was convinced I was meddling."

He cast a sidelong glance at me. "Are you meddling?"

I set my jaw stubbornly. "About as much as *she* was, interfering with my sister's happiness." *About as much as you have been.* I left those words unspoken, but they hung heavily in the air between us. "I sent Grace to Willowbark so she can speak to Holden and they can choose what *they* want."

Fitz's expression was sober. "Unfortunately, their choices don't only affect them."

"But there are other ways to form alliances," I retorted.

He sighed. "I know. And I will do all in my power to find one that will satisfy Willowbark. I don't want to fight with you," he added. "Please believe that I truly thought your sister was indifferent, that this plan for an alliance would leave her unaffected, or I never would have moved forward toward it without consulting you. I am not against you, Elle. I am on your side, always."

I swallowed against the burning in my throat and turned to him, throwing my arms around his neck. "Then let's quarrel no more. Please. And promise me this: no more secrets."

Fitz chuckled, the sound rumbling in his chest as he gently pulled back, his fingers caressing my chin to lift it and study my face. "I promise. There have been enough secrets and tricks between us to last a lifetime." As he released me and we walked onward, he threaded his fingers with mine and cast me a sidelong glance. "You seem unusually prone to dangerous encounters, Blackford. Have there been any other threats recently that I should know about?" His gaze was piercing, already anticipating my answer.

As I relayed the ghost's attack from last night, Fitz's jaw tightened. Though I didn't like to be the cause—however indirectly—of his distress, I couldn't help but admire his sharp profile in the moonlight as I walked alongside him.

"Then we shall visit the library next, and I'll see if I can send this restless spirit on," my husband declared when I'd finished my story.

"I think she was a mortal queen named Charlotte Berkley, married to Caedmon Ashwood," I explained, telling him of the journal entry I'd read. "It would explain her fear of my magic as well as her draw to me, a fellow mortal queen." I squeezed Fitz's hand. "You won't like this idea...but I'm not sure she will appear for you if she hasn't yet. Let me see if I can talk to her alone first, and then I can invite you in."

"The instant you're in danger," Fitz growled, "call for me."

"Of course. But you know you needn't worry too much. She flees from my magic."

"Are you ready?" Fitz asked, unable to smooth the concern from his brow as he scanned my face.

"I should be asking you that. You don't look ready," I teased.

Fitz's mouth set into a firm line. "I know you're capable with your magic, but you cannot send a spirit on. I hate to linger out here while you go in alone. She's already harmed you once." He brushed his thumb over the back of my hand.

Standing on my tiptoes, I pressed a kiss to his mouth, but Fitz seized my waist and pushed me against the wall. He drew out the moment, his tongue caressing mine before he trailed his lips down my neck, leaving me breathless.

My husband smirked. "You needed a proper kiss."

"I'll only be a few minutes before I call for you."

"Yes, but we just stopped quarreling. Besides," he added with a wink, "why would I not take every opportunity to kiss you breathless, Blackford?"

Smirking, I concentrated until I had summoned a small cluster of glowing silver spheres that resembled starlight hovering above my palm. A thrill of power coursed through me. Holding it between us proudly, I took a moment to admire the way their glow danced in Fitz's eyes before I turned toward the library door. "See? I'm ready."

Dismissing my magic, I pushed the door inward. It groaned as it opened, and a breath of chill air caressed my face, making me shudder. Dim starlight filtering through the windows cast long shadows that loomed like wraiths. I shut the door carefully behind me, giving Fitz one last reassuring glance. Every muscle in his body was tense and ready to spring if I gave any indication of needing his help.

"Charlotte Berkley?" I whispered into the darkness, searching the aisles and every nook and cranny for an indication that the queen's spirit had become corporeal and was wandering the space. "Queen Charlotte?"

Silence reigned, stifling and ominous. My skin prickled with the sensation of being watched. She was here—I was certain of it. I just couldn't see her.

My mouth dried. I could brave an attacker I could face, but an unseen one that could sneak upon me? That was terrifying.

"I read your journal entry. I'm also a mortal who fell in love with a fae prince destined to take the throne," I tried. "I know that the witch, Deidre, didn't want you to marry Caedmon."

At the witch's name, a hiss filled the air and a cloaked and hooded form appeared opposite me. "Curssssse that witch!" the ghost cried, seizing a book from a nearby table and hurling it toward me.

Ducking, I held my hands up, palms out in surrender. Perhaps I'd made a mistake in mentioning Deidre so soon. "My name is Elle Blackford, and I'm married to Prince Fitz Ashwood. I'm here to help you."

But the form vanished. "Charlotte?" I called, spinning in a circle as I surveyed the library. My blood rushed through my veins and the hairs on the back of my neck rose. I could feel the ghost watching me again, waiting.

There was no sign of her.

I waited for her to strike. For unseen hands to smash me into the wall, to hurl another object at me, or to seize me by the neck.

Silence reigned. "Charlotte?" I called once more. "Let me help you. My husband can send spirits on. If you aren't ready to move on to the afterlife, you can find rest in the glade of souls."

A creak in the floor made sweat bead on my brow, but I saw nothing. Perhaps it had only been the groaning of old wood.

Maybe.

I swallowed against the dryness of my throat. Waiting. Watching.

Shadows seemed to move in my periphery, but each time I turned, I found nothing but darkness. Once, I was certain I saw a pair of eyes with bloody tears trailing from them. I strained to hear her whispers.

At long last, I released a breath and let the tension in my body ease. "I'll visit another night," I promised, and left the library, resigned.

"Elle?" Fitz asked when I slipped out the door, electricity already flaring around him, its light dancing in his eyes. "You took so long. Are you hurt?" His voice was guttural, promising retribution if Charlotte had laid a finger on me.

I shook my head. "She didn't linger. She was too afraid."

He sighed. "I won't rest easy until she's left the castle." He took my hand and led me down the staircase. "Until then, we will lock our doors and be vigilant."

"I won't let down my guard again," I vowed.

We had just descended the steps and entered the hallway when a form darted from the darkest shadows. I froze, a bolt of fear shuddering through me as I imagined what sorts of awful news a servant might be bringing, to run to us like this in the dead of night.

Fitz's instincts were faster, noting that something wasn't right. He stepped in front of me, but before he could call on his magic, the figure lifted its arm, driving a dagger straight into my husband's chest.

CHAPTER NINE

My scream of fear and rage shattered the stillness of the night, bringing a host of guards racing toward us.

Even with the dagger's handle still protruding from his chest, blood pumping from the wound and spilling across the rich carpet, Fitz was instantly in motion. His magic was swift—a burst of lightning that enveloped the stranger and pulsed through him so intensely he didn't even have a chance to scream. His body collapsed to the floor, mingling with the growing crimson pool. The acrid scents of singed fabric and burnt flesh mingled with the tang of blood, and my stomach roiled.

Fitz teetered on his feet, his breathing ragged.

"Fitz," I murmured, tears springing to my eyes as I turned to catch him. He slumped against me so heavily I stumbled under his weight.

Chaos ensued as guards rushed us and took him from me, carrying him down the hall. Several shouted for servants to fetch a healer. Someone bade Fitz to stay alert. Another demanded to know how an assassin had entered the castle unhindered. A group charged through the halls with weapons drawn, searching for more imposters.

I couldn't focus on anything. Nothing made sense. I was weightless, watching my own body from somewhere above as it trailed stiffly after the guards transporting Fitz to our rooms. My vision was blurry; the world was distant. My chest was hollow and my body numb, disconnected from everything and everyone.

As the guards burst into our quarters and laid Fitz upon our bed, an alarming amount of blood soaked through his jacket, even with the dagger still lodged in place. His dark hair had escaped its tie and hung loosely about his shoulders, while his glazed eyes blinked at me before drifting shut.

He was so pale. Too pale.

Somehow, a coherent thought clicked into place in my mind. "Please, send for Kinsey," I begged, seizing one of the guard's arms. It took me a moment to register that it was Ronan, his sympathetic eyes studying mine, taking in the blood coating my hand.

"He's already been summoned," Ronan told me gently. "Did the attacker harm you, Your Highness?"

"He stepped in front of me. Fitz saved me." My voice shook. "If it hadn't been for me, he might have reacted faster and not been hurt." A tear slipped down my cheek.

"It wasn't your fault," Ronan interjected before I could ramble further. "Asking for Prince Fitz's first instinct to *not* be protecting the ones he loves would be asking for His Highness to not be himself."

I grimaced, knowing this was true. It was one of the reasons I loved Fitz so much.

Kinsey arrived at that moment, striding toward the bed. "Water and cloths," he said gruffly, glancing toward a pair of servants huddled nearby, who immediately straightened and hurried to fetch the items. His eyes shot to me, the usual warmth in their green depths replaced with only business. "Get her out of here." He nodded at Ronan and the other guard.

"What?" My voice was hoarse. "No. Let me help, let me—"

"There's nothing you can do right now. Please, Elle. Listen to me. I need to focus."

I relented at his softened tone, letting Ronan and the other guard—who, now that I glanced her way, I recognized as a newer one named Rose—lead me out to the adjoining sitting room. They sent for servants, who brought me a basin of water and a cloth to scrub the blood from my hands. I sobbed as I watched the water turn pink, my body trembling with the horror that I was washing away my husband's blood. So much blood.

Someone pressed a mug of tea into my hands, urging me to drink. I tried to sip at it as I sat by the fire, staring into the dancing flames, but I could focus on nothing but the sounds filtering in from the bedroom. Fitz's occasional groan, a sound that brought me slight relief even if it was pained, for it meant he was still alive. Kinsey's hushed words, saying things my mortal ears couldn't make out. Servants bustling in and out of the room, fetching items as Kinsey requested them. Bandages. Fresh cloths. Water. Vials of unfamiliar liquids and herbs.

Finally, after a long, miserable night of waiting and fearing, Kinsey himself opened the door, pausing to lean against the frame wearily. Early morning light silhouetted his slumped figure as he studied me. His sleeves were rolled to his elbows, his hair was in disarray, and his eyes were shadowed. "He is stable, but he won't fully heal. I can't knit the flesh back together."

Icy claws pierced my chest. "What?"

"Something is wrong," Kinsey admitted. "The blade struck his lung and nicked his heart. I can't heal the damage. There is resistance to my magic, as if some other magic is at play. As if the dagger was cursed."

The word *cursed* rang in my ears. Air snagged in my lungs. The world tilted and swayed around me, even though I was seated and still.

"I'm not sure what we can do. What I can do. But I'll keep fighting," Kinsey whispered. "You can go to him now. He's awake. But..." His unspoken, grief-laden words hovered between us.

He might not pull through.

My pulse thrummed with urgency as I followed Kinsey into the bedchamber, studying Fitz's form, his chest rising and falling with labored breaths. The bloodied bedclothes had been replaced with fresh ones. Fitz's soiled jacket and shirt had been removed, his bare chest clean and bound in tight bandages. To see my powerful husband struggling for life cut me to my very soul. I could not bear it.

I dropped to my knees at the bedside, grasping his hand and reaching up to brush his hair off his clammy forehead. He shifted to study me, his gaze still hazy. "Blackford," he murmured. "The sight of you gives me strength." He tried to smile, but the effort was weary, a pale shadow of his usual grin.

"You're going to be all right. You'll recover." Despite the way I'd hoped to reassure him, my voice cracked. "You *must*."

Fitz squeezed my hand, his eyes fluttering closed as he grimaced. "Of course. I dare not disobey you, wife."

I prayed that was true.

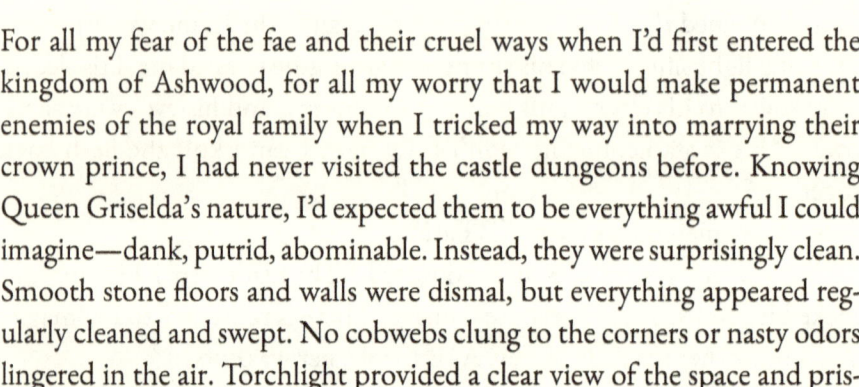

For all my fear of the fae and their cruel ways when I'd first entered the kingdom of Ashwood, for all my worry that I would make permanent enemies of the royal family when I tricked my way into marrying their crown prince, I had never visited the castle dungeons before. Knowing Queen Griselda's nature, I'd expected them to be everything awful I could imagine—dank, putrid, abominable. Instead, they were surprisingly clean. Smooth stone floors and walls were dismal, but everything appeared regularly cleaned and swept. No cobwebs clung to the corners or nasty odors lingered in the air. Torchlight provided a clear view of the space and prisoners that appeared, if dismal or hopeless, at least well-fed and bathed. The cells all had cots supplied with fresh bed linens.

Fitz and his siblings' doing, I'm sure, I thought proudly. Of course my husband, Holden, and Cordelia would all have insisted upon humane treatment of their prisoners. Even if they later suffered atrocities at the hands of their spiteful, bloodthirsty queen.

I drew a deep breath as I approached the cell that housed Queen Griselda herself. Even in the dungeons, she sat primly on her cot with her hands in her lap, looking as composed and proud as if she were preparing to hold court right here.

The corner of her mouth curled in a gloating smile when she saw me. "I wondered when you'd show."

"What do you mean?"

"My people don't want to accept you as their new queen, do they? Are they protesting my punishment? Rioting in the streets?"

I scowled. "It's much too soon for anyone to even know your fate yet, Your Majesty," I snapped, letting her title sound like an insult on my lips. "That's not why I'm here. I need to know anything and everything you know of a family curse."

She blinked, unable to conceal her surprise. "A curse? I have no idea of what you speak."

"A family curse cast upon the Ashwood family generations ago by a witch named Deidre."

Griselda narrowed her dark eyes. "I know that name, but I've never heard of a curse."

I chewed my inner cheek, musing. "What about all the ill fortune that has befallen your family?"

She raised her eyebrows. "You speak of my husband's assassination and Cora's murder? Those were not the result of ill fortune or a curse. They were the consequences of being royal and powerful. You'll learn, soon enough. It carries constant risk. You must be strong enough to bear it." She smiled slowly, all teeth and cruelty. "Though if you are killed, there will be no chance at all to bring back your mortal soul."

I ignored her. "Fitz is wounded. A would-be assassin stabbed him in the chest, and Kinsey cannot fully heal him. He said it is as if the dagger had been cursed." My stomach swooped just speaking the words.

Griselda went still, the color slowly draining from her face. Her expression was carefully neutral as she studied me. "So you think if there is a curse, there is a way to break it and save Fitz."

I nodded.

"Don't focus on a family curse cast years ago," she snapped. "Learn about the assassin and how they carried a cursed blade. Have someone with knowledge study the weapon." Her eyes sharpened on me. "Bring it to me. Let me see it."

I hesitated, but Queen Griselda was no fool. She knew Fitz wouldn't keep her locked in the dungeons forever and that another attempt on my life would cost her dearly. And, however much she despised me, she loved her son. She would fight to save him.

"Very well. I'll have a servant deliver it to you so you can study it. Send word if you discover anything at all."

With that, I strode away. Though I was willing to explore every option, I was convinced that Charlotte Berkley's spirit was the key to all of this.

I had more journal entries to read—and a ghost to visit.

CHAPTER TEN

I spent the morning curled up beside Fitz, who slept deeply thanks to a vial Kinsey had made him drink, and reading Charlotte's journal entries.

Meeting King Caedmon was a happy accident. With only a fortnight to try to find a way to avoid my forced betrothal to the witch's son, I decided the only help I'd find would be from another immortal. After bidding my loved ones goodbye—or at least, spending what I feared would be my final days with them before slipping away so they wouldn't try to prevent my leaving—I'd ventured into Ashwood, determined to find a fae who would help me.

I hadn't gone far into the forest before I encountered a handsome fae. At first, I was wary, but he'd seemed surprised and uncertain, not at all like the cocky, dangerous fae I'd been warned about.

"What are you doing here?" he'd asked, his rich brown eyes widening as he took in my plain mortal dress and curved ears. "You must be careful."

"A fae, warning a human?" I could not help but smile. "Are you not here to steal me away or make some ill-fated bargain with me?"

He shook his head earnestly. "No. I don't like what my kind does to yours. Once, the gods entrusted us with magic and long lives to protect this earth and all the beings in it. But now we immortals abuse what we've been given and treat those we deem lesser than us very ill. It's wrong."

"It's not as if the gods intervene," I murmured sadly.

"That's why it's up to us to choose to do better," the fae said firmly.

His sincerity warmed my heart, making me wonder if I could trust him. If he could help me.

"What's your name?" I asked softly.

"Caedmon. And yours?"

"Charlotte," I said. "I've come to Ashwood seeking help, actually." And so, I explained what had happened with the witch.

Eagerness lit Caedmon's eyes. "I believe I can help you."

The following entries chronicled the succeeding days, in which Caedmon and Charlotte determined the only way to break the magical power Deidre's vow held over Charlotte was to seek the help of another witch. Using Caedmon's status—after he hesitantly revealed to Charlotte that he was king—they'd scoured the royal library and spoken to countless advisors and nobles for information about other powerful witches, eventually learning of one in Willowbark.

Along the way, the two had fallen in love in a whirlwind romance. I couldn't help but find myself touched by their tender moments as Charlotte discovered Caedmon's unusually gentle nature. The pair reminded me a little of Grace and Holden.

When we arrived at Louella's cabin, Caedmon drew her aside. To this day, he hasn't shared the price he paid to compel Louella to break the bind Deidre had upon me. I fear he sacrificed something very dear, but all he ever tells me is that it was worth it. For me.

As soon as we returned to Ashwood, we were wed. The very next day marked the day that Deidre was to fetch me in the mortal world, and I awaited it with dread...but nothing happened.

Days passed. Weeks. Months. And then years.

Caedmon assured me that Deidre would not want to defy her king.

But I still have nightmares of those greedy eyes and sharp, yellow teeth.

The next entries were more mundane, detailing daily events and important moments in Charlotte's life as queen. Important decisions made. Moments celebrated. The births of her children. And then I came across one with scrawling handwriting, as if she'd written hastily or with a weak, shaky hand.

I followed my heart, and I'm afraid it will be the end of me. Though it has been years, I fear I have brought evil upon myself...and perhaps upon my dear husband as well. How did I ever allow myself to grow complacent, to believe I could escape this fate in a world full of curses and vengeance and wicked, powerful magic?

The letters won't stop coming. None of the messengers can ever describe the author who gave the letters to them—likely they have been spelled—but I have no doubt. Their threats are clear.

Deidre means for me to pay at last.

My stomach churned when I turned the page, only to find Charlotte's handwriting had been replaced by another's. Her son. His entries gave no clues regarding his mother's or father's fates, but it was easy enough to guess.

The spirit in the library with her bleeding face made it clear Charlotte had met a terrible end, and the curse she spoke of had to have been placed upon her—upon her entire family—by the witch she'd defied.

Desperate days and nights passed in a blur. Kinsey and I spent as much time as we could keeping vigil over Fitz—the healer draining himself of energy and magic as he constantly tried to stitch my husband's wound back together, only for his efforts to come undone. His endless work was the only reason Fitz didn't bleed out, but we both knew this could not go on forever.

"Every time the wound reopens, it happens faster." Kinsey swallowed, his expression grim as he spoke to me in the adjoining sitting room while my husband slept. "Soon my magic will have no affect at all."

I visited Griselda more than once, only to learn she could find nothing suspicious about the dagger and had sent it to some of her advisors to study. They reported the same thing: it was but an ordinary weapon.

Just as I had suspected.

Each night, I visited the library, trying to gain Charlotte's trust so I could ask her about the letters she'd received and the curse that had been placed upon the Ashwoods. After reading in her journal that she'd loved chamomile tea, I left a cup of it out on one of the tables, hoping the scent would comfort and entice her to approach me. Another night, I sat in an armchair, paging through a book and sharing stories from my life in the mortal world in hopes it would remind her I was human. By the third night, the whispers started again, and Charlotte slowly crept out from the shadows.

"You can help me?"

I didn't move quickly, not wanting to startle her into either attacking or fleeing. "Yes."

"Your name is Elle?"

I nodded slowly.

"You are human? You fell for a fae too?"

I nodded once more. "And you can help me too," I said carefully. "For if I don't find a way to help him, he will die."

"Help," she repeated. "How? I can do nothing. I am lost and need help. Please." She closed her eyes and kept saying the word like a chant, like she still wasn't fully aware that she was speaking to someone. Like a prayer she'd recited for so long, it had become a part of her, an unconscious habit to while away her lonely years. "Please please please."

I stepped closer. "How can I help you? What can you tell me of the curse and how you died?"

But the word curse had the spirit reeling back. In a breath, she vanished.

After several days, I ordered Griselda to be released from her cell so she could visit Fitz. It wasn't right to deny her this chance to tend to her son—or to say goodbye, if the worst were to happen. She, Cordelia, Kinsey, and I scarcely left his side during daylight hours. Kinsey barely left at all, having to be reminded regularly to eat and drink and sleep. Dark circles took up permanent residence beneath his eyes.

Fitz spent more time asleep than conscious. His breathing became more labored as the days passed; his complexion turned paler the more often his wound reopened and pumped out blood. His appetite was small, and though he tried to hide it, his glazed eyes and weary smiles betrayed how weak he was becoming.

"We must send for Holden," Cordelia said one evening, her voice cracking. Blue eyes red-rimmed, she slumped in her chair at Fitz's bedside and glanced at her mother.

Even proud, stern Griselda looked haggard and uncertain. Without a word, she nodded.

My stomach flipped. I couldn't watch Fitz slip away. I couldn't give up. I refused to say goodbye.

That night, I slipped away after Griselda and Cordelia had reluctantly retired to their own rooms and a servant forced Kinsey to sleep for a short while in our sitting room. I pressed a kiss to Fitz's temple, watching him sleep. Every uneven breath was painful to watch, like a dagger driving deeper and deeper into my own heart.

If only I had been the one who'd been stabbed.

When I entered the library, I sensed something was different. Charlotte was pacing the aisles, wringing her hands. She whirled at my approach, but rather than flee, she drew hesitantly nearer. As if she'd been waiting for me.

"You can help me?"

Again, I nodded.

Bloody tears leaked from her eyes as she blinked, but I refused to flinch at the gruesome sight. She coughed into her hand, and when she pulled it away, scarlet stained her palm. "Show me your magic."

I froze. "What?"

"Show me. Show me you mean no harm."

Ever so slowly, I raised my hand and called on the light that mimicked the stars, sending the tiny orbs dancing about my fingers.

Charlotte's eyes latched onto the glow, and for a moment, raw terror leaked into her expression and she seemed to forget everything about me. "Are you a witch?"

I dismissed my starlight, enshrouding us in inky blackness. "No, I'm a human. My fae husband shared his power with me. Did King Caedmon not do the same for you when you wed?"

"I-I don't remember."

In the darkness, with only the dim moonlight filtering through the windows to help me, I squinted to study Charlotte's expression. "But you remember Deidre, the one who hurt you. Please, could you tell me about her? Do you know what she did to you?"

There was a long pause. The weight of Charlotte's stare was oppressive. "Why do you want to talk of the witch?" she demanded at last.

I swallowed thickly. "My husband is dying, and I believe it is because of something that witch did long ago."

Charlotte reared back, her hood falling away to reveal dark curls and a glowering expression limned in silver moonlight. "She's abominable." She halted suddenly, frowning. "Though I...cannot remember what she did." She wrung her hands, her eyes growing distant. "But I know her name. She hurt me. Her magic hurt me."

"Was it a curse?" I whispered. "Did she curse you?"

The ghost scrunched her face. "She is the reason I'm trapped here. The reason I cannot return to my love, cannot find him—" Her voice broke as she choked on a sob.

I hesitated, wondering if Charlotte knew she was a ghost and all her loved ones were long dead. Did she long to find the glade of souls and eventually move onto the afterlife, where her husband was probably already waiting for her? Or did she think she was under some other sort of curse, trapped in a lost state? Without the ability to soothe her or help her pass on myself, I didn't want to be the one to reveal the truth to her. "I'm sorry," I said instead. "You wrote in your journal entry that you feared for the entire Ashwood family. I want to break the curse she placed on you. To make things right for the Ashwoods."

"There's no bargaining with her!" Charlotte's voice rose to a shriek as she shoved the table over, toppling books with a splintering crash.

My heart leapt to my throat. I didn't think it would matter if I explained that I wasn't sure if Deidre was even still alive. "I'm not her," I reminded her gently. "I mean you no harm."

Now that my vision had adjusted further to the darkness, I noticed how pale her complexion was, how dark the shadows beneath her wild eyes appeared. What I could see of her skin was spotted with dark blotches as if it were bruised all over, though they didn't look quite like bruises either. It wasn't obvious what had killed her. An illness? Something inflicted by Deidre's curse?

"Did she curse all of the Ashwoods? Please try to remember."

For a long moment, Charlotte paced the floor. Blood pooled in her eyes and dripped from her nose, leaving spots behind her steps that she didn't appear to notice. My stomach curdled. I could only imagine what she must have suffered in her final hours. At last, she spun toward me. "Letters. I recall words sent to threaten us. Caedmon and our children and me. Deidre said..." She coughed, blood dribbling down her chin. Again, she didn't seem to mind, as if she couldn't feel it any longer. "She said that since I'd broken my vow, I'd pay the price." Closing her eyes, she drew a breath and then recited:

For robbing me of my future,
I'll rob you of yours.
For denying my son an heir,
I'll give yours grief to bear.
And for breaking your word,
I'll make good on mine:
With a curse upon you and your line.

I considered the words. "So she's fond of rhymes," I said wryly. "Did she give any further details about the curse? Is there a way to break it?"

But Charlotte shuddered, the blood thickening and coating more of her face. It streamed from her eyes like tears and poured forth from her ears, staining her cloak. She choked on a strangled cry, her face twisting in agony and rage, and it no longer seemed as if she knew who I was or what was happening. She was lost in some long-ago moment, maybe seeing Deidre in place of me. She screamed and lunged. I leapt backward, calling on my magic instinctively in the same breath.

Lightning flashed and clouds swirled, obscuring Charlotte's vision and giving me the chance to dart for the door.

CHAPTER ELEVEN

My tutor was humming and pouring herself a cup of tea when I entered the library early the next morning.

"Elle," she said, her green eyes alight with welcome. "I hope the reason for your visit is a good one?" But her smile faltered as she took in my rumpled appearance. I could only imagine how awful I looked after so many sleepless, anxious nights. "I take it there has been no improvement."

She hurried to me, leading me toward an armchair and settling me in with a steaming cup of tea and a scone. Though I tried to protest, my stomach rumbled, and I realized I couldn't remember the last time I'd had a full meal. I'd nibbled on food servants had offered, but I'd done it all in a daze, hardly conscious of such basic needs as hunger, thirst, or weariness.

I ate and drank as I relayed Kinsey's lack of success and his fear that something had cursed Fitz. Then I explained how I'd discovered who the spirit in the library was and how Charlotte Berkley and the entire royal line had been cursed.

"Do you know anything about this witch?"

Setting down her cup, Dahlia scrunched he nose. "Deidre served the royal family for many years, until, for reasons never recorded and long forgotten, she tucked herself away in a cabin deep within the woods. There she lived with her son and hardly ventured out. Anyone who sought her help had to find her first."

"Could a curse she placed on an entire family be broken?"

"It's a law of magic," Dahlia said, staring down into her mug of tea thoughtfully. "When formed, a curse must also contain a way to break it. It is a limit the gods placed upon the witches' magic, thankfully. But the witch is able to choose how the curse can be broken, and word the solution in such a way that it is difficult to decipher. *Or* the solution can be obvious yet painful. Curses are rare, because they usually can only be cast after a great sacrifice is made. For Deidre to curse an entire family? She must have given up a lot. I doubt she would have chosen an easy solution to such a curse."

"Is Deidre alive now?"

"No one seems to know what became of her. The latest accounts I heard spoke of fae who ventured deep into the forest to make requests of her and never returned. It's possible that, in her old age, she became angry and violent, more prone to slaying her visitors than granting their wishes. Witches and warlocks are so powerful that not only does their magic leach away their beauty and youth, but also it steals their minds. Usually, near the end of their long lives, they grow unpredictable and a bit mad."

A chill swept over me. "Do you have any idea where her home might have been? Where it could still be, if she lives now?"

My tutor frowned. "Elle, a hag like Old Mother Deidre is extremely dangerous."

"If I don't try to do something, Fitz will *die*." My voice broke. "I need to find out how to break this curse. Charlotte barely remembers her past life, and I don't have any time left to waste trying to help her do so."

Dahlia studied me for a long moment. "I worry if Deidre lives, she will not share the way to break the curse with you, or will kill you before you can attempt to lift it. Why must it be *you* who seeks her? Why can't I try? Or send a solider. There are many powerful men and women who serve the Ashwood family loyally. You could send an entire host of soldiers."

I swallowed thickly. "I cannot sit idly by while he suffers. If we fail to break the curse, I want to know it was because I did everything in my power to break it. That it was my failure and mine alone. That's the only way I can live with...that I can consider living..." Trailing off, I blinked back my tears. I couldn't even say the words. Couldn't comprehend a life without Fitz.

Dahlia sighed. "Very well. I can accept that, even if I don't like seeing you risk yourself." She turned and approached her cabinets, opening one and pushing teacups and saucers aside to reveal a set of shelves hidden in the back, all laden with glass vials brimming with varying shades of liquid. Withdrawing one filled with something the shade of amber, she held it up for me to study. "I try to keep a supply of useful potions on hand, all acquired from our finest potion masters who made these using the best ingredients from our landing, drawing on its magic. This one will transport someone to something or someone that is hidden."

My eyes widened as she offered the vial to me. "How does it work?"

"I'd wait until you're out in the forest, where other fae magic is less likely to interfere. Here in the palace, anyone even using a simple glamour could affect the potion's magic and cause it to go awry. Then, you'll uncork the vial, drink the potion—all of it—and then speak the name of the one you seek aloud. She went by Old Mother Deidre."

"And then?" I prompted.

Dahlia shrugged. "If it works, you'll know what to do."

"That's it?" I said, frustrated and perplexed.

"I've read about it, but I've never used a seeker's potion myself. It can be a bit unreliable, but when it works, it can transport someone to whom or what they seek almost immediately."

"And how will I return when I've finished?"

"The potion will only keep you there for a limited time before it'll return you to wherever you were when you drank it. I believe half of an hour."

Not long, but hopefully long enough. Mulling this over, I carefully slipped the vial in the side pocket stitched into my leggings. "Are you going to tell someone of my plan or force me to take someone to go with me?" I arched a brow at her.

Dahlia shook her head, her curls bobbing. "Unfortunately, the potion won't take more than one. You have to drink all of the vial's contents. I won't conceal what you're doing once you've gone, but no one will be able to more than guess where you are." Her expression turned solemn, more solemn than I'd ever seen it before. "Don't make me regret this, Elle. I'm trusting you not to get yourself killed or endanger the kingdom unnecessarily. If you fail, I'll likely be labeled a traitor. So if you refuse to worry about returning for your own sake, return for mine."

I started to nod, but Dahlia halted me by throwing her arms around me and pulling me into a warm embrace. Though she was shorter and smaller than me, her hug was fierce and comforting. "Be careful," she said, her tone gentler this time as she pulled away, blinking hastily.

"I will." I swallowed. "I promise I will."

Her eyes darted toward the window, studying the morning light. "When will you leave?"

I straightened. "As soon as possible. Before Queen Griselda or Fitz have a chance to miss me at another formal dinner or other event for the Willowbark royalty." I cringed. "Could you make my excuses to Kinsley for me? He will be the only one to miss me for a while, since I won't make our training."

Crossing her arms, Dahlia clucked her tongue at me. "What do you think I am—human?"

I rolled my eyes. "Oh, I know you can twist your words to make my absence sound like something else without telling an actual untruth. Besides, if this potion works, I shouldn't be gone long. I hope."

Crossing to the door, I had just opened it to leave when Dahlia's voice stopped me.

"Elle? Don't reveal who you are, if you can help it. Deidre won't cast any spells without a cost, and witches are known for their weighty prices. A mad one could ask for something heavier still. If she doesn't know who you are, perhaps it won't be terrible...but I'm afraid no matter what, she may ask something too great of you, something more than you can bear."

I scowled. "I can bear anything for Fitz."

When I returned to our rooms, I was pleased to find Fitz awake, and Cordelia and Griselda absent. Only Kinsey sat nearby, and when I asked for privacy, he slipped out into the sitting room.

Taking Fitz's cool hand, I cradled it in my own as I shared all I'd learned about Charlotte, the Ashwood curse, and Old Mother Deidre. "I'm going to find her and force her to share how to break the curse."

Fitz's expression was solemn. "Be careful, Elle. Hags' magic is different from ours. Unpredictable. Wild. Strange."

"I'll be wary."

A muscle jumped in his jaw as he threaded his fingers with mine. "If you do not return by evening, I'll burn this whole forest down to find you," he said gruffly. Even in his weakened state, he managed to sit up enough to pull me into an embrace.

"You need not resort to anything so extreme, dear husband. The forest is our home. I promise to come back to you, safe and whole."

"I know you will." Fitz brushed a hand through my hair and then pressed a kiss to my temple. "My strong, brave Blackford."

CHAPTER TWELVE

Bundled in a wool cloak to fend against the chill, I rubbed my mittened hands together and watched my breath steam in the air. Overhead, the clouds were dreary grey, heavy with the promise of more snow to freshen the piles I trudged through.

Out here in the forest, spring and summer both seemed a long way off, but I knew the months would pass in the blink of an eye. If we backed out of our alliance with Willowbark, we might have them to contend with at the height of their power this spring as well as Ravenheart in the summer. But I hardly had room in my heart to worry about that anymore, not now that Fitz was hurt. A world without Fitz was unbearable, unthinkable. I couldn't consider it. Couldn't even imagine that I might fail. I had to break this curse, and I had to believe that would be enough to save my husband.

I withdrew the vial Dahlia had gifted me, studying its contents. If the gods were watching, if any cared about the fate of those living on the earth they'd created at all, I prayed they would let this potion work.

I uncorked the vial and gulped its contents in one draught. The liquid was cool yet bubbly, warming me from the inside out like a fae wine. Unfortunately, its aftertaste was bitter, filling my mouth with a flavor that reminded me of dirt and regret. I swallowed thickly, wishing away both the taste and the sense of foreboding stealing over me.

I lifted my voice, speaking clearly into the stillness of the forest. "Old Mother Deidre."

For a tremulous heartbeat, nothing happened. The trees creaked and swayed in a breeze, stirring up swirling snowflakes from their branches that dusted my hair and cloak. Something crept through the underbrush nearby, and I scanned the area hurriedly, my thoughts darting toward my magic in case some fae monster or other horror revealed itself.

Instead, the world seemed to shift around me. I blinked, shaking my head to try to dislodge the sense of vertigo overtaking me, until I realized the forest seemed...different. Ahead, the trees were taller, wider, and more ancient. Their snow-laden branches were gnarled and rough. I turned, wanting to see if I could catch a glimpse of the castle behind me, and instead found myself facing a stone cottage.

If I hadn't known to be wary of its occupant, it would have been a cozy home. Smoke curled from its chimney, filling the air with the scent of a merrily burning fire and stew. Though the curtains were drawn, golden candlelight shone dimly through them. The entryway was swept clear of snow, and the door was painted a cheery green that stood out in the browns and whites of the winter forest.

Creeping forward, I drew a deep breath and knocked on the door.

For a long moment, nothing happened. I ground my teeth, wondering if Deidre would simply ignore me. Surely a witch wouldn't be able to resist a chance to trick a poor mortal into paying a hefty price for a spell...or would she? My lungs constricted as this new fear overtook me—that instead of having to make a sacrifice for Grace, I wouldn't be able to do anything for her at all. I'd never considered the possibility that Deidre might refuse me altogether.

Then the door swung inward, and a hunched old woman blinked up at me with narrowed eyes. Her grey hair swept down nearly to her knees, even in the tangled, frizzy state that it was. Her dress was simple and patched, as if she'd been mending it on her own for quite some time. Her gaze darted from my head to my toes as her lips drew into a scowl. "A filthy mortal wandering Ashwood Forest. Meek mouse, scurrying about until something far more vicious and cunning scoops it up with claws and fangs. What do you want?"

Ignoring the singsong way in which she'd spoken, either in warning or in a threat, I said: "Old Mother Deidre, I've come to request your help."

She scoffed, showing off her yellowed, crooked teeth. "If you know who I am, you know I do not perform charity. Go back to your mortal world, before you perish on your foolish mission." Her eyes darted about the forest, as if I weren't already keenly aware of its dangers, even without spirits freely roaming its borders. "Trees have eyes. Clouds have ears. Shadows have teeth." She chomped her own together.

"Not charity." I straightened, hoping I appeared more confident than I felt. "I'm willing to pay."

Turning up her nose, she sniffed as if I disgusted her. "Trinkets, shiny things, baubles all! I doubt you have anything I want." She began to push the door shut, its hinges creaking out a warning that my time to convince her was drawing short. "Let me melt and descend into the dust in the place where my thoughts speak to me."

I shoved my boot into the entryway, blocking the door from shutting completely. "It's regarding the Ashwood curse!"

Instantly, the witch froze, her eyes widening and her lips cracking into a devilish smile. "Interesting," she crooned. "What does a mortal know of this curse?" She gave me a once-over, her shrewd gaze roaming over my body as if seeing me for the first time. "A descendant of the unfortunate Queen Charlotte, perhaps?"

My heart thundered in my ears, but I refused to react. She didn't need to know I was the new Ashwood princess. "No, I am not of the Berkley or Ashwood families," I said, calmly. "But I've learned of the royal curse, and let's just say that I'd like to have some leverage."

Deidre cackled. "Ah, a cunning one. I suppose you mortals have to be, to survive in or near our world." She opened the door wider, welcoming me in at last.

As I stepped over the threshold, I relished the warm air wrapping me in its embrace even as my skin prickled with unease. Earthy scents wafted from within: coming from both the herbs bubbling in a cauldron over the fire and dried flowers hanging in bunches from the rafters. Along the wall, shelves boasted an assortment of leather tomes, jars, and a collection of bones. Some appeared small enough to belong to a mouse, while others looked disturbingly like they could have once been part of fae or humans.

"What do you hope to gain from this leverage you want against the Ashwood family?" Old Mother Deidre asked, her hunched form hobbling around me to approach the fireplace. She lifted a poker and glanced over her shoulder at me, eyes gleaming in the flickering flames. I had a sudden fear that she would have another lapse of sanity and attempt to run me through with the poker. I was stronger and faster, but I was no fool. I knew her magic would make her a formidable foe. I had no idea what this woman was capable of.

I lifted my chin, flashing a smile I hoped signaled confidence. The lie came easily. "Power. I want to leave a legacy that will outlast my feeble mayfly life."

I knew Deidre would empathize, and sure enough, she gave me a wide smile. "The mouse schemes to rise to the level of the owl. Hoot-hoot, have you feathers? A beak?" She tipped her head and showed me her yellowed teeth.

Before I could puzzle out if she wanted me to answer her nonsensical questions, she turned back to tend the fire, stirring it into a hearty blaze. "How did you learn of the curse, little owl?"

"I was a guest in the palace and encountered a ghost who spoke of an Ashwood curse and a witch named Old Mother Deidre living deep in the woods."

"Clever of you to find me here," she said with a cackle, lifting an eyebrow and studying me archly. "How did a mortal slip through the nets and ensnare the ensnarer?"

I didn't let her question make me stumble. It seemed best to let a grain of truth enter my next lie. "I made a deal with a fae for a vial of seeker's potion."

The witch cackled. "Dangerous business, making deals with immortals. Do you know the true cost yet, mmm?"

I set my chin stubbornly. "It's worth it, for what I will gain."

She continued to laugh. "And what do you want to know of the Ashwood curse?"

My pulse hiccupped. I could not fail. I had to be careful, had to wheedle the information out of her. "You're the one who set the curse upon them, are you not? Is it truly one that will make the generations suffer?"

Deidre stepped away from the fire and hobbled toward one of her shelves, lifting a human skull and studying it almost affectionately. "It has taken many Ashwood lives, and given great pain to many others. The current queen has already lost a husband and a daughter, has she not?" She tapped the skull with a bony finger. "And now another son is cursed to forever be parted from his true love, while the other will suffer an untimely death to separate him from his."

My lips went numb as I tried to conceal my horror and settle my expression into one of indifference. She already knew of the attack on Fitz, and she believed it would cost him his life. I tried to act confused. "An untimely death? For which prince?"

She fluttered her lashes. "The crown prince has already been struck by a furious member of the gentry, stabbed by a member of his own court. But that attack was empowered by my curse. That assassin will succeed because of it, for it is my magic that will keep the prince from healing." She growled. "For the ants and the rats and the spiders whisper to me. They tell me he fell in love with a human, that another mortal will become queen of Ashwood." Her glare was sharp, and a bolt of terror shot through me. Even out here, she'd heard the news? Was it possible she also knew who I was? "He will suffer greatly for that."

Throat thick, mind whirling, I pursed my lips to avoid asking a flurry of questions. Too many would make me sound concerned and give me away, if Deidre didn't already see through my deception.

"What do you hope to use as leverage, hmm?" She waggled her eyebrows. "Wanting the knowledge of how to break it? What makes you think I would sell that information so easily, when nothing gives me greater pleasure than to see that family suffer?"

"Because I can taunt them with the knowledge but not share it," I snapped. "I can humiliate them. I can tell them I have the key to end their suffering and to save the crown prince, and then I can lie about it. He will die anyway, for I will share the knowledge too late, after they have granted me what I want. A place among their nobility."

Deidre laughed. "You weave pretty lies, but that's not tantalizing enough, Princess Elle Blackford, wife of Crown Prince Fitz Ashwood. I know you seek to break the curse."

I lifted my hands, summoning storm clouds that coalesced in the shadowy corners of the cabin. Purple flares of electricity pulsed through the space in time with the rapid beat of my heart.

Smirking, Deidre waved a hand and dark, faceless forms–like shadows come to life–appeared at my sides, seizing my wrists and startling me into dismissing my magic. I ground my teeth, fighting to pull away from the shadow figures.

"How much more could I make the crown prince suffer before he dies, if he loses you too?" the witch clapped her hands together eagerly. "He could bury your dusty mortal bones before he joins you to converse with the grubs and worms."

"You'll risk his wrath," I growled. "Don't doubt that he would make you suffer. He would have his revenge."

Her eyes gleamed wickedly. "Ah, but he is weak and dying. And even if he does manage to wreak revenge, I will also have mine."

I gave another fierce tug, but the shadow forms' grips were like ice-cold vises, painful and constricting. Desperation clawed at my throat as I called on my magic again, watching flashes of electricity dance in my peripheral vision. "You want to see the Ashwood family suffer," I panted, continuing to struggle, "but you already had your revenge. Charlotte continues to suffer as a spirit, trapped in the castle. She is the one your ire is toward. We had nothing to do with her failed vow to your son."

"Bah! I hate all of you. Her husband, King Caedmon, was a proud sort, and their descendants have all been the same. I take pleasure in my revenge, and my suffering has not ended either. My line has ended." She bared her teeth. "My son is dead–executed at Ashwood hands."

I refused to let surprise show on my face. The storm clouds continued to grow in the corners of the cabin, but Deidre's focus was on me. "What did he do?"

"What did *he* do?" the witch snarled. "You mean what did those vile cretins do? They murdered him! They condemned him for being my son, out of fear of my power and what he might have inherited from me. The fae wield great powers, but they knew mine were formidable and I only hold allegiance to myself."

Taking advantage of her distraction, I called on the storm I'd summoned, making the clouds swirl about us thickly as lightning lanced in a dazzling arc toward Deidre. She cried out, sparks dancing about her form as she stumbled backward, but she did not even fall.

Then she lifted her chin and smiled. "Ah, little owl, you do have talons. What a delight to have a visitor who is no cowering mouse." She cackled. "Squeak, squeak! You'll die like one all the same, though."

Her shadow forms wrenched at my arms, forcing me to my knees. I swallowed bile as I glared at Deidre.

"If the creatures whisper to you about the Ashwoods and me," I said, "then perhaps you heard I tricked the prince into marrying me instead of my sister. All for his power." I nodded toward the clouds I'd let retreat toward the corners of the room again.

The hag licked her lips. "True, it was no love match, even if he fell in love later." She considered. "But did you also fall for him? That is the question. Have you truly come to me wanting to see him brought low? To taunt him and his family with the solution to the curse? They're haunted, yet they know it not. I am the manifestation of all their worst nightmares, and they do not even know to seek me out."

"Would it not be satisfying to know I could tempt them with a way to break the curse, only to never grant them the knowledge?" I urged. "We could bring them low together. I knew when I learned your story that you were an ally."

Deidre's narrowed eyes swept over me, assessing. Her shadow figures continued to hold me down like guards awaiting an executioner to approach and take my life. I met the witch's stare without yielding, determined to force her to believe me, or to at least consider believing me for a moment. Determined to make this work.

She blinked, and I drew a deep breath, waiting. Focusing.

"Mortals can lie." She sneered.

"If I betray you, could you not curse me in retribution? That would be more satisfying than killing me now, wouldn't it? Watching me suffer?"

Deidre tilted her head this way and that, reminding me much of the owl she'd called me. "Clever, but I see no reason to trust you. Perhaps you want to know how to break the curse to play the heroine and gain power that way, hmm? Why should I ever trust you, tricksy trickster owl-mouse? I see your beak. Your talons!"

She approached as if to deal a death blow, though she bore no weapon. I wondered what sort of other magic she would wield, and I braced myself, knowing I had no time to waste. "Of course," she went on, "perhaps I should let you live. For to break the curse will surely be your undoing." She cackled cruelly. "But first...something for your arrogance."

Deidre flicked her hand toward me as if wielding an invisible weapon. A dagger of shadow formed in the air and flew toward my face. I had no doubt that it would be as sharp as iron, but I was ready. Roots tore through the floorboards of her cabin, splintering wood and shooting debris and dust into the air. Deidre's dagger ricocheted off one of the thick roots, spinning end-over-end until it struck her in the shoulder. She shrieked as the roots wrapped around her torso, securing her arms at her sides. Blood soaked her side—her shadow blade was long and sharp, and it had left a deep wound.

Even her shadow forms released me, staggering back as they melted into nothingness.

"No mortal has ever wielded the power of the land to this extent," she gasped. "And you...you are not worthy. You are *no one*."

"Not no one," I said, rising and allowing myself a smug smile. "I am the rightful queen."

With a snarl, she squirmed against the earthy restraints. Another blade of shadow darted through the air, and I ducked. It struck the wall behind me and fell harmlessly to the floor.

"I have nothing to lose—no reason not to pay the price to curse you," Old Mother Deidre taunted, her eyes flaring with bloodthirsty glee even as I let the roots tighten about her. "But first, I'll give you what you want. The method of breaking the curse is hidden within the letters I sent to Queen Charlotte! Enjoy what you discover." She laughed with abandon.

Narrowing my eyes, I tossed her one last disdainful look before I turned on my heel and strode toward the door. "You won't live long enough to curse anyone ever again." Electricity was already thickening the air, tingling along my skin and making the hairs on my arms rise.

Deidre shrieked in livid protest as I darted outside, slamming the door so hard the entire cabin shook. I'd taken a mere two steps before I let the great storm clouds swirling over the hag's abode release their own fury. A single bolt of lightning–so loud it left my ears ringing–struck the cabin, making the wood burst into flame. It was so powerful, so vicious, that it was a roaring fire in an instant, tearing through the structure and leaving nothing but charred ash behind.

I didn't wait to see the full effects of my destruction. Holding my breath, I closed my eyes and willed myself back at the castle. Back into Fitz's arms.

Back to a way to rescue him, before I lost him forever.

CHAPTER THIRTEEN

When I opened my eyes, I was in a new area of the forest, the reek of ash and smoke replaced with the scents of freshly fallen snow and the crisp, old leaves from the past autumn. I wasted no time in racing back toward the castle, rushing past servants who glanced curiously in my direction and racing up the stairs. I burst into Fitz's and my quarters to find Kinsey still at his friend's bedside, seated in a chair and hunched over in weariness. He glanced up in surprise at my hurried entrance.

My husband's eyelids fluttered at my approach, his blue gaze fastening on me.

"Fitz," I gasped, terror gripping my heart.

He reached for me, threading our fingers. His grasp was clammy and cold, but his fingers were still strong. "You're back," he murmured. "You're safe."

"She confessed to cursing your family," I choked out. "But I have to search for the way to break it and save you. And we haven't time to waste."

Kinsey perked up, his brow scrunching in confusion, but he did not interrupt our conversation.

"There's time. I draw breath still," my husband said with a hint of humor to his voice, but when I met his gaze, I noticed a glimmer of doubt in his eyes.

"I have to find the letters Deidre sent to Queen Charlotte."

"Did she do anything else?" Fitz's tone was dark. "Threaten you or curse you or demand some awful price?"

I lifted my chin. "She tried to, but she's dead."

Fitz smirked. "My devastatingly dangerous wife. Of course she is."

I cast him a sidelong glance. "You never told me that your power could extend to controlling the land–or that mine could."

His eyes widened. "It's rare for a royal to possess such powers before they've taken the throne. And it's unheard of for their mortal spouses to share in that ability."

My lips curled upward in satisfaction, my heart warming at the pride in his expression. I hesitated, but only briefly, allowing myself this one moment. "I had a feeling, given how powerful the magic you share with me is already, that if I focused enough, the land would gift me the magic to call on it too...that it would let me control more than the night and the storms. Just like it did for you when you stopped your mother."

"I shouldn't be surprised the land has accepted you so fully. It is because of our bond."

I wanted to melt at his words, to relish this moment and enjoy that we were on good terms again. But I couldn't linger, as much as I hated to leave my husband's side. "Take good care of him, Kinsey."

"Where are you going this time?" Kinsey's words were sharp, like a stern brother concerned for my well-being. Perhaps he scented the tang of ash and smoke on my clothes.

"Nowhere near as dangerous as before."

"Where do you intend to start searching?" Fitz asked. "Charlotte's rooms now belong to my mother, and she's occupied them long enough to discover any of the secrets those quarters contain."

But I was confident. "The very place her soul cannot leave."

Kinsey trailed me out of the room, leaving Fitz to drift into much-needed sleep and giving me a chance to voice my concerns outside of my husband's presence. "How is he?" I whispered.

My friend's eyes were shadowed from lack of sleep and worry. He shook his head. "The wound is reopening faster than ever now. I won't pester you with questions about this curse...but whatever you're up to, Elle, please be careful." His eyes darted back toward where Fitz slept.

"Does anyone else know? Have Cora or the queen been to see him? Has anyone sent a message to Holden?"

Kinsey shook his head. "Until the castle has been secured, he didn't want them wandering off to meet him. He has guards watching the rooms for the entire family—including yours—and asked that no one leave their quarters tonight. He didn't want them to worry or risk themselves."

I frowned, though I wasn't surprised. "Did the guards find anything?"

"No one else. They still aren't sure how the assailant snuck past our defenses, but they confirmed he was a nobleman. A disgruntled one who repeatedly made it known that he didn't want Prince Fitz to take the crown."

I nodded, relieved to hear they hadn't found anyone else and praying it meant everyone else would remain safe. "Thank you, Kinsey." I touched his shoulder before I bid him a quick goodbye and slipped away.

Daylight was already fading, the sky painted a golden-grey hue as I entered the library. Dust motes danced in the last rays of dusk, and I blinked against the brightness after creeping about the dark castle. The air felt lonely and still without Charlotte's presence. I could still sense her on some level, but it was different—a spirit watching unseen instead of a corporeal body roaming about the aisles. But she would likely be here soon.

I didn't hesitate. I strode to the place where I'd seen Charlotte crying the night she'd first drawn me here. The floorboards creaked beneath my boots as I strode between the shelves, scanning book spines for any hint of letters that might be tucked within any of the pages or a journal that might have belonged to Charlotte, containing more information about her life and the curse. But my search among the shelves was fruitless. I pulled book after book out, flipping through pages, running my fingers along the binding to search for a way papers could be tucked within them, and searching for journals that might contain Charlotte's handwriting.

Every moment, I pictured Fitz lying in bed, his complexion too pale, his breathing too labored.

I couldn't lose another loved one to an early death. I couldn't.

My own breaths grew shallow with my growing panic as the sun's rays became stronger, warming me as I stood in their glow.

What if the hag had been taunting me with something worse than a difficult way to break the curse? What if she'd somehow made it unbreakable? What if she had been taunting me with a fruitless search?

The floor creaked and groaned as I paced, fretting and wondering if I should scan every single shelf and book within the library. That would take ages.

I began taking stacks of books to a nearby chair and paging through them until the words began to blur before my eyes. Until I began to second-guess myself. Perhaps there was another reason Charlotte haunted the library. My heart sank with despair. It could take months to search the entire castle and uncover its secrets. Years.

At some point, I must have drifted off, for a voice startled me awake. I straightened in the chair, finding my neck stiff and uncomfortable. A book lay open in my lap. Morning light streamed through the windows, highlighting Dahlia's curls as she tilted her head and studied me.

"Elle, it's good to see you've returned safely. But what are you doing here?"

I rubbed at my eyes, hating myself for giving into sleep, though it was no surprise. I hadn't slept since the night before Fitz had been attacked, and my use of magic against Deidre had drained me. Maybe that was why Charlotte's ghost hadn't even disturbed me last night, though frustration welled within me all the same. I'd hoped she could help me in some way, and now I'd lost another night, another chance to speak with her.

"I think I know where the solution to breaking the curse is," I blurted, before explaining everything to her. "Please, help me find Deidre's letters."

Dahlia's brow furrowed. "First, let me send for breakfast. You look awful."

I opened my mouth to protest, but realized I was parched and famished. When had I last eaten or drank anything?

She shot me a knowing look. "You cannot save Fitz if you run yourself ragged and collapse." She rang for tea and breakfast, and then made me eat my fill and drink two cups of tea before she would even consider letting me lift a book again.

We divided the space into sections, each taking our own rows. The sounds of flipping pages and muffled footsteps filled the air as we hunted, the clock in Dahlia's cozy corner where we studied ticking away the moments.

As morning turned to afternoon, Dahlia found me in one of the aisles.

She sighed, brushing a curl away from her face. "We should ask for help. The princess, your family...even the queen may wish to search."

As Dahlia swept over to her armchair and her pulley to ring for a servant, the sounds of hoofbeats pounding against the courtyard cobblestones reached my ears. I raced to the window and gazed outside, watching a carriage decorated with Ashwood's insignia pull toward the stables. I waited eagerly until I saw Grace and Lina exit the carriage and approach the castle.

Stifling a cry of relief, I exclaimed to my tutor that Grace had returned and rushed from the library, running at an un-princess-like pace through the halls and hurtling down the stairs. I met Grace in the entrance, not even allowing the servants greeting her a chance to take her cloak before I threw my arms around her neck.

"Elle," my sister cried, embracing me tightly. "We encountered the messenger bringing Holden the news on our way back. I'm so sorry. Is there anything I can do?"

"Come with me," I urged. I turned to Lina, who pulled me into a hug as well. "You too, if you can. We can use all the help we can get."

By the time we returned to the library, the rest of my family, as well as Cordelia, were all gathered with Dahlia. I explained what I'd learned of the curse and what we were searching for.

As we began to scour the aisles together, Isabel frowned, glancing back at Grace. "What do you mean about being on your way back? You did not return with Prince Holden?"

In the time that Grace had been away, I'd told my family of our hopes, and Isabel and Bridget had both swooned over how romantic it was that their sister was rushing off to confess her love to the prince. They'd daydreamed of Grace and Holden meeting in one of the spring kingdom's orchards, glistening with icicles as the sun dipped below the horizon, or spending a cozy evening near a fire, stargazing through the window and sharing the deepest wishes of their hearts.

Pursing her lips, Grace shook her head. "Lina and I were never permitted in the Willowbark palace. We were always turned away, as if the servants had been ordered to send us off." She swallowed. "I suspect Holden knew we were there, and knew it wouldn't be right to see me when he is betrothed."

Before I could protest, Cordelia set the book she'd been flipping through down and set her hands on her hips. "That's absolutely untrue. My brother adores you, Grace. If anything, I'm guessing the queen of Willowbark suspected something—or maybe my mother sent word ahead of you not to let anyone from Ashwood speak with Holden. She found out the very night you left."

I mused over Cordelia's words. I had no doubt that, with her influence, Griselda had ordered a messenger to ride out to Willowbark with such a warning. My blood boiled at the thought. "Where is she now?" I demanded of Dahlia.

"She didn't want to leave Prince Fitz's side just yet. She ordered some servants to begin searching other areas of the castle."

Good, I thought. Though all help was welcome, I was relieved to hear my mother-in-law wasn't about to join us in the library when I was this furious with her.

Another long hour passed. At last, I returned to the first aisle I'd inspected, the one where I'd found Charlotte that first night. Something drew me here, despite my failed search earlier. Surely there was a reason Charlotte had chosen this place, specifically, to linger and cry. Even if her spirit couldn't remember why, something tied her to this spot.

When the floor groaned beneath my feet again, inspiration struck. Sinking onto my hands and knees, I ran my fingertips along the wood boards, feeling the grooves and cracks until my hand caught on something. One of the boards lifted at the corner when I tugged. Heart in my throat, almost afraid to hope, I pried the floorboard loose. Dust floated through the air, but in a small rectangular space lay an aged stack of letters. Out of the damaging sunshine, the ink was still legible, showing what must have been the witch's scrawling handwriting. I paged through the messages carefully, not wanting the brittle papers to crumble. There were the threats Charlotte had written about, along with the curse she'd recited to me.

Seating myself on the floor, I laid the letters out side-by-side around me, analyzing each word, each sentence. Father and I had enjoyed solving various puzzles like this back home. This one wasn't too difficult, when I knew what to look for. Italicized words in each letter spelled out a sentence. Calling to Dahlia, I asked her to fetch me pen and paper so I could write out the answer.

Everyone gathered around me, holding their breath as I worked.

When I finished, I sucked in a heavy breath, setting the pen down. My head spun.

Voices echoed around me as everyone peered at the words I'd scrawled out, but the sounds rang in my ears nonsensically. All I could focus on were the words swimming before my eyes. The solution I didn't want to see.

No wonder Old Mother Deidre had laughed.

I was doomed to lose Fitz, with or without the curse.

CHAPTER FOURTEEN

y mouth dried. Grace grasped my hands, helped me to my feet, and led me to one of the armchairs clustered before the fire. "Oh, Elle," she breathed, her eyes brimming with unshed tears.

Dahlia, Cordelia, Mother, and the rest of my sisters gathered around my chair.

I squeezed my eyes shut wearily as the damning words repeated in my head:

The Ashwood curse will only die when an Ashwood chooses to surrender life, when family blood is spilt upon this ink. Then the curse will vanish as these words disappear from this page.

"Surely there's a loophole," Bridget said, her face scrunched into a troubled frown as she scrambled for a solution. "There always is with the fae."

But when she turned to Dahlia, my tutor shook her head, her face pale. "I cannot think of one. Curses are powerful things that require powerful sacrifices to cast, and powerful sacrifices to break." Tears swam in her eyes.

"It's another way for her to have her revenge against our family." I laughed mirthlessly. My chest was hollow. "This way, if anyone ever did break the curse, that person would still go without love. Without a future. Without life. Just what she felt like she and her son were cursed to face."

Mother seized my hand as I attempted to stand on unsteady legs. "You cannot be thinking–cannot consider..." She swallowed. "*Elle.*"

I squared my shoulders. "I am an Ashwood by marriage, am I not?"

Immediately, my sisters, Cordelia, Mother, and Dahlia all burst into conversation at once, demanding and pleading that I not even consider the very idea that had latched in my mind and would not let go.

For there was no other way. No other choice.

To sit back and let Fitz die was unthinkable. I knew he would be furious, but if he were in my place, I knew he would do the same.

My sacrifice would hopefully also grant Grace a chance at happiness—and, I prayed, not at the cost of an alliance with Willowbark.

Isabel threw her arms around my neck and clung to me, weeping into my shoulder. Sniffling, Bridget knelt beside Grace, taking the hand that my older sister hadn't already claimed.

"Surely there is another way," Maggie said, seizing the letters from where I laid them out on the floor and poring over them with Dahlia. "Bridget has to be on to something. This can't...it's not right!" She swallowed, her throat working.

"It's unthinkable!" Mother's voice trembled as she tried and failed to conceal her emotions.

Cordelia was silent, as if the talk of death had brought up the pain of her time as a ghost, restless and lost and afraid. She shook her head at me, her eyes silently warning me that such a choice could not be unmade. Unlike her, I wasn't immortal with a chance to be brought back. And returning to life was only an option for immortals who were wrongfully killed, not ones who willingly chose to sacrifice their lives.

I scrubbed a hand over my face. "I need to see Fitz." When Mother cast me a worried look, I added, "That's all I plan to do for now."

For now.

But when I chose to break the curse, I knew I wouldn't be able to face my family again. They'd try to talk me out of what I knew I had to do. I couldn't live without Fitz, not when I had the power to save his life.

Gathering the letters from my sister and Dahlia, I turned for the door. I was once again assailed with embraces and pleas before anyone let me slip out of the library. I needed space—to breathe, to think, to grieve.

When I reached our quarters, Kinsey was still keeping vigil at Fitz's side while my husband slept. "Any change?" I asked, though I knew it was too much to hope for that.

Kinsey sighed and shook his head. As I settled into another chair and cradled Fitz's hand in my own, I relayed everything I'd learned about the curse to Kinsey—except the fact that I'd found out how to break it. I couldn't bear the thought that Fitz might overhear me. Though I wanted to bid him a proper goodbye, I knew he would try to stop me. He'd be furious when he recovered, but the kingdom needed him more than it needed me.

And I couldn't face a world without him.

"Could I have some privacy with him?" I asked my friend after I'd shared my story.

Kinsey agreed, leaving to lie down on a settee in the sitting room while I turned back to my husband.

I brushed a dark lock of hair back from his forehead, blinking against my gathering tears. "I love you more than anything," I whispered, watching the ragged rise and fall of his chest. "Please keep fighting. Please wake up." A tear slid down my cheek, and I leaned forward to brush a kiss to his brow.

He was unresponsive, lost to the world as his body failed to fight against his wounds. My stomach clenched, and I reached down to squeeze his hand. How cruel that this was to be our goodbye. How cruel that we'd only just found one another, just set aside our less-than-favorable first impressions and prejudices to fall in love, and already we were being forced apart.

As I left my rooms to sneak out of the castle, cold regret seized me. I'd let my family believe that I would wait and grant them one last farewell.

But in this moment, I felt like a coward, far too weary to bid goodbye to one more person. Everyone would be livid, and yet I feared if I had to face their tears again, I would lose my nerve.

And that wasn't an option.

Instead, I went to my old quarters, the ones I barely spent any time in since Fitz and I had grown close. I rang for Lina and sank into an armchair by the empty hearth in my sitting room, staring into the grate.

"Oh, Elle," my friend cried as she burst into the room. "I only just heard from one of the guards on my way up or I would have sought you out sooner. How are you?" She shook her head as she settled near me. "That's a ridiculous question. Never mind me. Can I fetch you anything? Tea? Something stronger?"

My tongue cleaved to the roof of my mouth. How did I tell my friend goodbye? Unable to find the words and not wanting to face her pain or attempts to dissuade me either, I fell into her arms and let her hug me.

"The glade of souls," I choked out at last. "Dahlia said it moves. But...if a mortal has a strong tie...could they find it?"

Lina pulled back, pity etched in the lines of her face before she managed to smooth it away. As I suspected, she thought I was planning on a way to cling to Fitz a little longer, even beyond the grave. "Elle, mortals die if they cross into the glade. Dahlia probably didn't tell you before, knowing you couldn't find it. Maybe Prince Fitz's magic would let you now, since you share a portion of his, but you don't have his spirit magic, so I don't know. But it's not something you can try, even if it did work. You would become a permanent resident. Mortals are not meant to find it until death claims them."

Closing my eyes, I inhaled sharply and nodded. I didn't have to hide my pain. Knowing what I had to do didn't make it easy.

"No matter what happens, though, I'm here for you," Lina whispered, her hand resting on my shoulder. "I'm so sorry."

"You're a good friend, Lina." My voice cracked with emotion. "You know, I think I need a walk to clear my head. I need some time to be alone and breathe some fresh air." I smiled sadly. "I don't want anyone to come looking for me. If someone asks, please tell them I went to my rooms to be alone and that I'm not to be disturbed."

Forcing an answering smile, Lina nodded. "Whatever you need."

As soon as she left, I bundled myself in my boots, mittens, and cloak. *These won't keep your body warm once your soul has left,* I thought morbidly. A stubborn tear snaked its way down my cheek as I slipped out the double doors leading to my balcony and climbed out, much like I'd once done when escaping from Fitz's quarters to search for Father's spirit.

That was the only thought that warmed me now: I would soon be reunited with Father.

Night gathered as I trod through the forest, the pooling shadows thickening until I could have sworn unseen eyes stared at me as I passed. But this time, I was no mere mortal venturing into a deadly forest full of fae and monsters. I had my magic dancing about me, a miniature constellation aglow with shades of violet, crimson, orchid, and indigo sprinkled with silver and gold. Anything that wanted to approach would see from afar that I wielded the crown prince's magic and was not to be trifled with.

As I crept forward, I regularly felt in my cloak pocket for the carefully folded letter, the one that bade me shed my blood upon its ink. My stomach clenched each time my mittened fingers brushed against the parchment, but my resolve did not waver. In my mind's eye, I saw Fitz, his bandaged chest rising and falling in a labored rhythm. I would pay any price to end his suffering and save his life.

Focused on my magic as I was, I could feel the gentlest tug urging me through the forest. It felt like a breath of wind pushing me onward with just enough insistence to instill confidence in my every step. My skin tingled from the magic's influence, and my heartbeat accelerated, reminding me that each pulse of blood through my veins, each inhalation of air into my lungs, each throb of my heart—every one was numbered. I clung to my happiest memories with my family and Fitz, with my friends I'd left behind in the human world and the new ones I'd made in Brytwilde. I would carry those with me into the afterlife until I could be reunited with my loved ones. They would have to strengthen me.

The crunch of another set of footsteps in the snow stopped me in my tracks. It seemed ironic to fear for my life when I intended to sacrifice it, but I couldn't perish before I accomplished my goal. Feeling for the dagger sheathed at my waist, I scanned the dark wood, searching for any sign of movement. I cursed my mortal eyes until a cloaked and hooded form emerged from among the trees, creeping up slowly, uncertainly.

When the figure pushed back its hood, Charlotte's familiar face peered back at me.

My eyes widened. "Charlotte? How did you leave the castle?"

Her form was corporeal in the night, and her expression seemed more certain and settled. The glazed look of confusion had vanished, and the blood that had poured from her face before was gone. She looked...almost alive as she studied me in the moonlight. "You're going to break the curse," she said softly. "I can feel it. It's loosening its hold on me, enough that I can seek out the glade of souls."

I envied the peace consuming her features, wishing I could feel the same. "Did you know?" I whispered, my voice breaking. "Did you know the cost?"

Tears pooled in her eyes. "Too late. She sent the last letter too late, when the curse had already made me take my last breath. I remember now—my spirit haunting the halls and seeing the letter delivered. A servant hid them." She frowned. "No—the messenger. Deidre's messenger, once she heard of my passing, concealed those letters. This was all a cruel game to her. My soul, even when I started to forget, stayed in the library, some part of me remembering where those letters were. But time passed, and the curse was forgotten. I couldn't find peace." She stared at me in awe. "Until you. Are you truly planning to step into the glade? Do you know what will happen?"

I nodded firmly. "You know it, or you wouldn't be here. Can you lead me to it?"

"Yes," Charlotte said softly, her footsteps dislodging snow and old leaves in the forest's underbrush as she moved ahead to guide me deeper into the darkness.

The forest canopy thickened, blocking out most of the sky's light, but my magic encased us both in a comforting glow.

"I must thank you for your courage," Charlotte murmured, glancing over her shoulder. "I don't know how long I've been trapped here as a spirit, but I assume it's been quite some time. What is your name?"

I didn't want to make small talk, but the distraction was helpful, so I shared my story with the former queen, explaining how I'd taken my sister's place in her arranged marriage to Prince Fitz and then fallen in love with my husband after all.

"I can see why you chose to do this and save him." Her look was sad. "I'm so sorry you have to be parted from him too soon. I understand your pain, though Caedmon and I had years and children together, not mere months. You've been robbed of far more than I was."

I didn't need the reminder, didn't want to lose myself to tears. If I let myself collapse and dissolve into sobs now, I would be delayed, and Fitz might be dead before we ever reached the glade. Instead, I remained silent as we waded through drifts of snow, the only sounds the crunching of our footsteps and my frosty breath.

Suddenly, the stillness of the wood was broken by distant sounds. At first, I wondered if it was a breeze stirring through the branches, but as we drew nearer, my skin tingled, as if the magic within me was responding to the spirits' presence. The sounds became clearer: they were murmuring voices. My heart quickened and my chest tightened. This was it.

Charlotte's expression grew eager, settling into more peace and happiness, almost giving her the appearance of life. But her corporeal body began to shift as we approached, melting away as if it had been nothing but an illusion. The closer we were to the glade, the more spirit-like she became.

Eventually, I was able to see the spirits themselves through the trees. The glade wasn't at all like what I'd imagined. For one, there was no snow nor sign of winter within it. It was as if it existed in another season, or in another world altogether. Though it wasn't the afterlife, perhaps it was connected to it, as a place where souls lingered peacefully as they prepared and waited to move on. A burbling stream, clear and sparkling in the moonlight, cut through long blades of grass gently waving in a breeze. Clumps of vibrant flowers and plants, many of which I didn't even recognize, were gathered along its banks. Souls of men, women, and children—fae, others of their kind, and human—clustered best the stream or strolled through the grass.

It was reassuring to see how many seemed to be cheerful and at peace, contentedly exploring nature or chatting with others. Only a few wept or kept to themselves, their expressions despondent or angry. Those were likely the ones still coming to terms with their deaths and their need to pass on, still attempting to find peace within this glade.

My stomach lurched as I paused at the edge of the forest, my head light and my body chilled. The land's magic pulsed through me, as if sensing my connection to Fitz's spirit magic even if I did not wield any myself. I shivered as I plucked Deidre's letter from my pocket, laying it atop the snow as I drew my dagger.

Steeling myself, I pressed the point of my blade to my fingertip, watching blood well.

Charlotte hesitated at the edge of the glade, studying me curiously. I wondered if she couldn't be fully free to enter until I finished my sacrifice, or if she simply wanted to witness the ending of the curse that had begun with her. I lifted my eyes to hers, watching her through my steaming breath. Then I grasped the letter again, holding it up to the moonlight.

I love you, Fitz. Grace. Mother. Maggie and Isabel and Bridget. Be strong without me. I'll wait for you. Tears stung my eyes. I ached to run back to my husband and lose myself in his embrace. I burned at the unfairness of being parted from him when I'd just barely met him. I broke knowing that Fitz would wake to the hollow grief I was leaving behind.

But I had no choice.

I pressed my finger to the ink, watching my blood stain the parchment, and stepped toward the glade.

CHAPTER FIFTEEN

"Wait!"

I paused mid-stride at Charlotte's cry and spun toward her.

"Read me the letter again. My memory is hazy on what it contained. How does one break the curse?"

Shaking my head in confusion, I walked back to where I'd dropped the letter, leaving it crumpled and bloodstained, growing damp with snow. She trailed after me, peering over my shoulder to read the words aloud.

"*The Ashwood curse will only die when an Ashwood chooses to surrender life, when family blood is spilt upon this ink. Then the curse will vanish as these words disappear from this page.*" She paused. "I am also of the Ashwood family."

My heart lurched with hope even as my mind rebelled. "But the curse claimed your life," I argued. "How could you choose to surrender it? You're already dead." But my thoughts were already spinning, already clinging to a way, in true fae manner, to twist the words to our benefit. The loophole in the cruel curse that would break it without breaking me.

"Do you truly think that surrendering yourself to the afterlife would satisfy the terms?"

"A soul, as eager as one is to move on toward peace and reunion toward other loved ones that have passed on, is always giving up something by accepting death and leaving this familiar world." Charlotte's words were somber, speaking to the ache in me that grieved for my father, not only because I missed him, but also because I hated all he had been forced to leave behind. "It's possible. We must try."

"You are close enough to cross into the glade of souls." But hope dimmed even as I spoke the words, frowning in the direction of the glade.

"And yet that is only a waiting place. You need help to move on, and I cannot be the one to help you pass into the afterlife. That is a power only granted to Ashwoods by blood, not by marriage."

But Charlotte's dark eyes were earnest and hopeful. "You were being led to the glade on your own by the magic you share with your prince," she insisted. "You are connected to the spirit magic. Your presence called to me and strengthened me." She gestured toward herself. "The more I'm around you, the less lost I become. You led me here."

I frowned, for it was quite the opposite.

"Your power did," Charlotte clarified. "I could not have guided you without it."

A chill rushed through me at her words as I recalled the way the land had responded to me, the strange connection I had to Fitz's magic that, before, had been unheard of for mortals.

"Elle," Charlotte continued, "you have a powerful bond with your husband. It is one I never let myself explore with Caedmon, because I feared magic too much. I didn't wield it freely as you do. I let that terror control me to the point that Caedmon died before he could help me to the afterlife." Tears shone in her eyes. "I'm confident you could do it for me. You can free me, and free our entire family in the process. You can break the curse and live your life with your husband. You can have the future Deidre wanted to deny us all."

I closed my eyes, concentrating on the tug I'd felt earlier, leading me to the glade before Charlotte had found me. The souls' voices and laughter reached my ears, blending into a soothing cadence. Power thrummed through my veins. I recalled how Fitz had dismissed a soul that had attacked me in the castle what felt like ages ago, before I'd let myself fall for him.

Opening my eyes, I gazed into Charlotte's face and instilled command into my words. "Leave the mortal lands and enter your eternal rest." Hope shone in Charlotte's eyes, and she swayed on her feet. "I release you into the afterlife."

Her face melted into a contented smile. "Goodbye," she mouthed, even as her seemingly solid body began to dissolve like mist, swept away on the whisper of a breeze.

For a moment, I stood staring at the place her soul had been, my heart pounding in my ears. The only sounds came from the souls in the glade and the creaking branches overhead.

She was gone.

I'd succeeded.

But had Charlotte's spirit satisfied the terms for breaking the curse?

Holding my breath, I scarcely dared to approach the crumpled letter. My blood pumped wildly through my veins as I approached and peered down.

The ink was still there, the words of the curse staring damningly back at me.

Nausea uncoiled and writhed in my gut like a snake preparing to strike. Body numb, I felt the hope drain from me, ebbing away like the last moments of my short, insignificant life.

I closed my eyes, fighting against the threat of tears. They would not serve me now.

There was nothing left to do but to follow Charlotte in leaving this world behind.

Trembling, I stepped forward, preparing to enter the glade.

"I knew it!" The snarling voice sent my heart leaping into my throat as I spun and searched the shadowy forest until my eyes landed on Queen Griselda.

Even trekking through the snow, trailing after me on her graceful fae feet, she looked elegant and queenly. Her brows lifted as her sharp gaze flicked between the glade and me. My stomach flipped and I reached for my magic on instinct, making storm clouds gather thickly around us.

"You're trying to claim the hearts of my son *and* my people," the queen went on, her blue eyes as sharp as a dagger. "Was it not enough to weasel your way to the throne by lying your way into a royal marriage?"

"How did you get here?" I shook my head, at a loss. "What are you saying?"

Queen Griselda stepped nearer, chest heaving with her furious breaths. "Word spread throughout the castle that you'd discovered how to break the curse, so I followed you. You've ruined enough, girl. You've shamed me. Turned my son against me so that he has condemned me to live out my days in wretched indignity. And now you want to be the heroine who saves our family from a curse? Who saves the future king's life? Bah!"

I gaped. "You said word spread through the castle? Did you also hear what sacrifice breaking the curse will require? Do you *know* what I'm about to do?"

She waved a careless hand. "Did I hear that you plan to give up your short, insignificant mortal life? Yes. Hardly a sacrifice when you exist for but a moment anyway. And yet you will be called a savior for keeping the crown prince alive. And then where will I be? He will mourn your life and treasure your memory and scorn me all the more, leaving me to rot in the dungeons or some dark corner of the castle while my kingdom forgets me."

"You're mad!" I cried, unshed tears stinging my eyes. "This isn't about you. I'm doing this so Fitz doesn't die." My voice broke.

Queen Griselda sniffed as if my statement had offended her. "And do you think *I'd* allow him to die? That you're the only one who would mourn his passing, or that would fight to see him live?" She shoved past me, nearly knocking me off my feet in surprise. "Get out of my way, girl."

I sucked in a shaky breath as Griselda drew a knife from her boot. "What are you doing?"

Calmly, she slit her palm open, seized the letter from me, and held her hand over the paper, letting her blood drip upon the parchment and mix with the faded ink. "Saving my son and preventing you from stealing my glory." She sneered at me before turning toward the glade.

"You're not a mortal..." I began.

She scoffed. "I gave up my spirit magic to Fitz and Cordelia, the next generation of Ashwoods. And..." Her nose scrunched as if she smelled something distasteful. "Apparently to you as well. Because of that, I am as susceptible to the dangers of stepping into the glade as your weak mortal soul. But it is my time. My crown has been stolen from me. I refuse to live out the rest of my days in shame. It is time to save my son and let him and all my people remember *me* as the one who saved them."

Warring emotions kept me rooted to my spot in the snow, my steaming breath obscuring my view of the queen as she lifted her chin proudly.

"Don't think I'm doing this for you," she added scornfully before I could open my mouth and express any gratitude. The idea that I wasn't about to die–that I would live to see Fitz again–was still forming, as if my over-exhausted mind could not quite grasp the concept. "Goodbye, girl. Treat my son and my kingdom well, or I swear to you, even from the afterlife, I will find a way to plague you."

And without a backward glance, she strode into the glade, every step as elegant and purposeful as if she were entering her throne room. I watched breathlessly as she faded before my eyes, her body seeming to dim as she became another spirit roaming about the clearing. Another soul waiting to move on to the afterlife. Another Ashwood queen leaving her kingdom behind.

I spun and raced back through the forest, snow crunching beneath my boots and my magical light encasing me in its glow to guide my way. By the time I reached the castle grounds, my breaths were ragged and my lungs were burning. I tore open a side door and charged into the hallway, nearly knocking over a startled servant. Lina.

"Elle! I was looking for you!" she cried. She seemed so distracted with whatever had her searching for me, that she didn't even stop to question why I'd been running through the halls.

My stomach lurched as I leaned against the wall for support, catching my breath. "Fitz?" I panted, terrified of what news she brought.

Lina threw her arms around me, nearly strangling me in her embrace. Pain lanced my heart, convinced she was comforting me. But then she breathed: "Kinsey said he's recovering,"

I yanked out of her arms. "I must see him!"

"Of course." Lina laughed. "Go, go."

Tears of relief nearly blinded me, and I dashed them impatiently away so I could race up the staircase and toward our quarters. By the time I darted through the door, I was beaded in sweat, my hair in disarray. Mother, my sisters, and Cordelia were all gathered in the sitting room, and turned in surprise at my entrance.

"Where were you?" Mother asked, her tone accusatory as she stood from an armchair, her eyes scanning my cloak and mittens.

"Are you well?" Grace demanded in nearly the same breath.

"I am, but I need to see Fitz." I threw off my cloak and tugged off my mittens, discarding them carelessly on the floor as I strode for the bedroom door. "Lina said..."

Kinsey opened the bedroom door, his smile wide and reassuring. "He's healing," he said as soon as he saw me. "The wound isn't reopening anymore. Nothing is fighting my magic. He will make a full recovery."

I nearly wilted with joy, but I pressed forward on trembling knees.

"I'm not sitting in my blasted bed when my wife is out there..." a familiar voice was protesting, when it trailed off and an arm shoved Kinsey aside.

My husband stepped forward, his bright eyes instantly locking on mine. He was fully dressed, the bandages around his chest hidden under his shirt and jacket. He moved with his usual grace and strength, without a hint of pain or weakness. "Elle, you're here." He pulled me against him, his erratic heartbeat a comforting sound beneath my ear. "Kinsey was trying to confine me here when everyone had told me you'd ventured off. I thought I'd have to burn down the forest after all."

I laughed through my tears as the door clicked shut softly behind me—Kinsey offering us privacy. "I'm sorry I wasn't here when you woke. I wasn't sure..." I swallowed. "I had to find a way to save you. I didn't know if it would work."

Fitz leaned back, gently grasping my chin between his finger and thumb to lift my face toward his and study my expression. His other hand brushed away my tears. "What would I have done in a world without you, Elle?" he murmured. "I would have been more lost than the souls that wander outside the glade."

"And I would be the same without you."

A bittersweet smile graced my husband's lips. "Then let us thank the gods that neither of us must face a world without the other quite yet." He drew me in for another embrace, crushing me to his chest as his other hand tangled in my hair. "Tell me how you broke the curse."

My heart skipped a beat, sorrow for my husband tainting my joy and relief at seeing him whole again. "I didn't," I whispered. "It would have cost me my life." Quietly, I recited the words I'd arranged together from Deidre's letters—the key to ending the curse. "Your mother followed me, Fitz. She chose to sacrifice her life instead."

Fitz glanced away, closing his eyes and breathing deeply. His brow furrowed as he processed the painful news. Though I knew his relationship with his mother was complicated—especially after she'd nearly killed me—she was still the one who'd borne and raised him. I knew he loved her. Knew that, in her own way, she'd loved him.

"I'm so sorry," I said, reaching out to tenderly brush hair away from his face.

My husband caught my hand in his, squeezing it as he turned back to me, forcing a pained smile. "She will be missed, but she gave me a gift, whether she wanted to or not. She ensured I didn't have to lose you."

I wrapped my arms around his neck and tugged him toward me. My whole world was the warmth of his body against mine and the caress of his lips as he pressed them to my temple.

CHAPTER SIXTEEN

The sounds of carriage wheels and horse hooves in the courtyard outside the castle made Grace pause with her forkful of egg halfway to her mouth, her arm visibly trembling. Then she blinked, her expression again settling into composure, and she took her bite. She continued with her breakfast as if all was well, when I knew she was both fiercely anticipating and dreading Holden's return.

Fitz and Cordelia had joined my family for breakfast this morning, apparently finding comfort with us in their grief. I could only imagine how they felt about their brother's homecoming and the news they would have to share with him.

Isabel stood from the table and darted toward the window of the breakfast room. "It's Holden! He's returned!"

"Sit down, Izzy," Mother admonished, but Bridget had already abandoned her seat to join our sister. Even Maggie had ceased eating to turn around in her seat and attempt to gaze out the window from her vantage point.

I squeezed Fitz's hand under the table in silent reassurance. He gave me a grateful smile before exchanging a look with Cordelia. They both excused themselves and slipped out of the breakfast room.

Throat tight, I stirred my food idly about my plate.

Sighing, Mother picked up her mug of tea and cradled it, as if inhaling its soothing scent would banish my sisters' unladylike behavior. "You know what news they must share with Prince Holden, girls. You should give them privacy."

I shrugged. "I don't think they mind."

Mother arched a brow. "It doesn't mean we need to forget the etiquette of where we came from. We live in a castle, Ellie." She cleared her throat, catching herself. "Elle."

My heart warmed to hear my mother remember my preferred nickname.

"They're embracing," Isabel said. "Oh, he looks as handsome as ever."

Maggie shot her a glare. "Is that what one should be noticing when he's missing his mother?"

"He's coming this way," Isabel narrated. "Fitz and Cordelia are following. Oh, he looks quite determined—he's running now!"

I reached for Grace's hand across the table. Our little sisters meant well, but they either didn't realize the extent of Grace's pain, or naively trusted that she and Holden would find a way to be together. Their lives weren't burdened with daily political complications and court discussions like mine had become—and, with her association with Holden—how even Grace's had become.

"Maybe he's coming here," Isabel said excitedly. "Surely he's missed..." Her words trailed off as she glanced back toward Grace.

"Don't be silly," Grace said with forced calmness. "He's an engaged man, returning from a visit with his betrothed. And she's a lovely, kind fae princess. They are a perfect match. Most likely he wants to pay his respects and take time to grieve his mother, and then return to the princess and what comfort she can offer him."

Isabel snorted in an unladylike manner. Mother pursed her lips but did not correct her again.

A knock on the door startled us from conversation. "Come in," Mother called.

One of the male fae servants whose name I hadn't yet learned hesitated in the doorway. "Prince Holden requests an audience with you."

Isabel smiled smugly. "With *whom*?" she asked pointedly.

The servant cleared his throat. "All of you?" It was a question, and his expression appeared bewildered. A moment later, it became clear why when Holden's impatient voice called: "Gods, Cedar, why such formality?"

Blanching, Grace pushed back her chair. "I feel a headache coming on. I think I need to retire to my rooms."

Isabel spun around as Grace stood to leave. "No, no, stay, Grace!" She seized our eldest sister by the wrist.

Before Grace could voice her protest, Holden burst into the room. His expression was frantic, his shirt collar wrinkled as if he'd been tugging upon it, and his hair wild, like he'd repeatedly run his hands through it.

His wild eyes fixed on Grace—and only Grace.

Silently, Fitz and Cordelia slipped in behind Holden, glancing between him and my sister.

"I'm so sorry for your loss," Grace began, but he shook his head, circling the table.

"I am sorry too, but that is not why I am here. I cannot wait another moment without speaking to you of this. It's tormented me the entire trip back home. Please forgive me," he murmured, and dropped to his knees before her.

Grace gaped, frozen in place.

"I didn't know you were in Willowbark," Holden went on. "And before that, I didn't realize the extent of your feelings. If I had, I never would have let anyone convince me into that engagement. I certainly never would have left your side. I thought it was a sacrifice I alone had to make, that I alone was the one who must suffer. Can you forgive my ignorance? I could hardly believe such an angel could love me, and so I was blind to your feelings."

Grace stared. "H-how did you learn of them?" she stammered.

Isabel grinned mischievously. "Did you think the royals are the only ones who can send messengers? Our friend Daniel was happy to oblige me." She fluttered her lashes.

"He reached me right before I departed, back when I thought I was returning to a gravely wounded brother," Holden affirmed. He studied Grace as if they were the only two in the room, and I felt suddenly embarrassed to be witnessing their exchange. "I adore you, Grace Blackford. You are the only one I want, the only one I love. I don't know if you can forgive me..."

"Of course I forgive you," Grace interjected softly, her eyes flooding with joyful tears.

Holden reached for her hands, cradling them in his own as he continued to kneel before her. "You are too good."

"But what about Princess Laila and the alliance?"

"She understood. I broke it off with her before I left. Both she and the crown prince formed a different alliance with me—a blood bond."

Fitz broke his silence, his eyes alight with worry. "What? Those are highly risky, Holden—you know this."

Holden cast him a glance before turning back to Grace. "Being with you is worth any price, Grace. And it's not as if Fitz or any of us plan to attack Willowbark. We all signed oaths in blood."

"If anything changes and any one of us harm Willowbark and therefore break your oath," Fitz growled, "you will be afflicted with a slow, painful death."

"Nothing will change." Holden's voice was certain.

Fitz swallowed back his uneasiness. "I hope their word is good and they won't find a loophole to force us to break the alliance."

Holden shook his head. "My time with them has assured me they are good people. I trust them, and they trust me." He looked up at Grace. "And now that I've broken free of that betrothal, I can't waste another moment. Grace, would you do me the honor of becoming my bride?"

A tear escaped, slipping down my sister's cheek. "Are you sure now is the time?" she asked hesitantly.

"Now is the perfect time to ask," he insisted. "Losing my mother has only made it clearer to me how important it is for me not to lose one more moment. I need you to know how I feel, that I want a future with you and only you."

Grace shook her head, not in answer, but in disbelief. Her smile was radiant. "Holden, I've been yours since the first night we met. I'm sorry you didn't know it sooner. I love you with my whole heart—"

But Holden had already leapt to his feet, taking her into his arms and interrupting her with a kiss.

Isabel and Bridget giggled, but Mother and Maggie shot them disapproving looks.

"We will give you privacy," Mother announced, ushering us all—even Fitz—out like naughty children. But I didn't miss the smile stealing over her face, the peace of knowing another of her daughters had found such overwhelming happiness.

CHAPTER SEVENTEEN

I t was a day of mixed emotions as Lina bound back my hair in a tight plait and lowered a black veil over my face to match my dress. In the fae world, black was still a color of mourning, but clothing was not as plain as what the grieving wore in the mortal world. Here, I was adorned in a midnight dress of velvet adorned with bolts of vivid color to mimic autumn leaves. It was a way to honor our land, and with it, the former queen who'd ruled over it.

Hand-in-hand with Fitz, I joined the royal procession of family members and guards winding out of the castle and into the forest. Hosts of citizens awaited us for the funeral proceedings already, their heads bowed respectfully. Everywhere there was black—black ribbons wound through horns and antlers, black swaths of clothing, and even black paint tracing intricate patterns across faces or over arms and chests.

Though Griselda's body had literally melted away when she'd stepped into the glade, there was a coffin in the center of the clearing where we'd gathered. There, mourners could approach and drape offerings across it. Petals, leaves, ribbons, dried flowers, little baubles and trinkets that I supposed had meaning to the givers that I did not understand.

Holden, Cordelia, and Fitz took turns speaking about their mother, sharing only the good. Focusing on her wisdom, her determination to protect and strengthen her kingdom, her power, and her love for her family. I stood respectfully at Fitz's side, my feelings in a tangle: grief for him, relief for myself and any Ashwood citizen who'd suffered her cruelty—Lina especially, though she refused to speak ill of Griselda now that she was dead—and nervousness for the ceremony that would soon follow.

Before I knew it, we were kneeling in final respect, ignoring the bite of cold and the dampness as we sank into the snow, and then lighting a funeral pyre. I soaked in the warmth as we gathered close, watching the dancing flames. Fitz slipped an arm around my waist and tugged me against his side.

"Thank you for this," he murmured, kissing my cheek. "I know you had no love for her, and I don't blame you. She treated you terribly. But thank you for supporting the part of me that grieves and misses her."

"Fitz, you don't have to thank me. I'm your wife." I leaned my head on his shoulder. "I'll always be here for you."

Fitz smiled and closed his eyes, as if relishing my nearness. "Thank the gods for that."

"Elle, I've never been so happy in all my life, and it makes me feel terribly guilty." Grace collapsed onto her bed wearily. After the dreary business of Griselda's funeral, we'd left the Ashwood siblings to themselves, letting them remember and mourn their mother alone. I'd retreated to my sister's room, cherishing this time with her and reveling in her joy with her.

"I feel awful for Holden, though I can hardly be sorry that the queen is gone." Her brow scrunched. "We want to be married soon. I asked Holden if he'd want to wait, but he insisted he does not."

"How soon?" I lay on the bed beside her, eager to hear every detail.

"Very, I think. We don't want an extravagant wedding." She paused, hugging herself and smiling dreamily. "Oh, Elle, I can hardly believe it, that he loves me and wants me to be his wife."

"I can! How could he not love you?" I turned on my side to face her. "I'm truly happy for you."

She sighed. "I'm so overjoyed. Fitz is healing, the curse is broken, and Holden loves me... Other than the loss of their mother, everything feels like it is finally as it should be. How could we be so fortunate?"

"By overcoming tragedy and fighting for what we want," I said firmly.

"It's done," Fitz murmured that evening, tugging off his shirt and sinking into the chair before the fire. He stared into the hearth, his gaze distant. "Cora and I met her spirit in the glade and sent her on. Even Holden was able to stand at the edge and speak to her."

My eyes burned with unshed tears. "I'm glad you had the opportunity for final goodbyes and to see her find peace," I whispered, leaning over the back of the chair to wrap my arms around him. "What do you need now? Tea? Or do you have an appetite to take dinner in our room?"

Fitz raked a hand through his hair, letting it fall loosely to his shoulders. "Sit with me."

I walked around the chair and perched upon his lap. He held me tightly in his arms, breathing deeply as he continued to stare into the fire. "Would it be all right if I shared my best memories of her with you? The ones where she wasn't so cruel or arrogant?"

"Of course." I ran a hand through his hair, cradling the back of his neck and leaning into him.

And so we held one another as Fitz told me stories of a motherly queen who'd taught her son how to play chess, who'd read books to him by the fire, who'd given him gifts and praised him when he excelled in his studies. One who'd encouraged and believed in him even as she was stern and demanding, expecting great things from her heir. I listened to it all with rapt attention, enjoying this glimpse into Fitz's boyhood.

At last, we took a light dinner in our rooms and then fell into bed, again enjoying one another's nearness. I clung to Fitz even as I drifted off to sleep, thankful to have my husband healthy and whole.

Soft knocking at our front door startled us from a deep sleep. Half-awake, Fitz's arms tightened around me before he seemed to realize a threat hadn't woken us. I blinked blearily into the darkness, wondering who would be waking us in the night.

I groaned, reluctant to leave the warmth of our bed and the closeness I savored with my husband, tucked safely against him. But the rapping continued. Slowly, we sat up. When I pulled back the bedcovers and swung my legs over the side of the bed, Fitz drank in the sight of my bare legs.

"It's cruel to be woken in the middle of the night to the sight of you and not be able to savor you," he said meaningfully.

My cheeks pinked. "You've seen me many times."

"And did you think I'd tire of your beauty? I'm convinced you'd put the goddesses to shame."

I glanced away, my blush deepening. "You flatter me."

"I speak the truth, Elle," he whispered, climbing out of bed and pulling me into an embrace. He pressed a kiss to my neck, my jaw, my lips...

"Fitz." It was Holden's voice in the hallway, low yet annoyed. "I can hear you talking. Whatever you're saying...or doing...can wait."

Sighing, Fitz broke our kiss, tugging his discarded shirt from last night over his head and approached the door. I trailed after him.

"Dress warmly and meet us outside by the pond," Holden said as soon as Fitz cracked the door.

Fitz frowned, but before he could ask his brother about his strange request, Holden had already slipped down the hall.

My husband and I bundled ourselves in warm clothes, boots, mittens, and coats before slipping through the quiet castle, encountering Cordelia, Mother, and all my younger sisters on the way. Bridget and Isabel whispered together, wondering why we'd been summoned at this hour.

We trudged through a fresh layer of snow along the path leading to the pond, which was covered in a layer of glistening ice, shining silver in the starlight. Holden waited for us by the pond, dressed in an elegantly embroidered jacket and pants. Lina and Dahlia were gathered nearby, their breath steaming in the night air as they leaned toward one another to talk. As soon as we approached, they broke into smiles and Lina darted away into the forest.

I opened my mouth to ask what was going on, but Dahlia turned to us with outstretched arms and a warm smile. "Welcome to the wedding of Holden Ashwood and Grace Blackford."

CHAPTER EIGHTEEN

G race stepped out from among the trees, looking resplendent in a lacy white gown adorned with delicate beads in the shape of leaves and flowers. A delicate veil hung from her hair, but rather than covering her face, it was thrown back so we could see her wide smile and the glow in her eyes. Lina held the trail of Grace's gown with her good hand, beaming nearly as much as my sister.

And Holden... I nearly teared up when I saw the way his eyes glistened as he stared at his bride, blinking to contain his emotion.

When Grace approached, he clasped her hands in his and leaned in close to whisper to her. It made my sister flush and wipe at her own eyes, and my heart warmed to see them so full of joy. Of course they'd chosen to be married now, in secret under this frosty, velvet sky. They were not about to let anyone else meddle in their affairs or steal their happiness again. No advisors or nobility could protest. By the time the members of the Ashwood court learned of their union, they would already be wed.

"Thank you for being here to bear witness to this union, made before the gods and Grace and Holden's loved ones," Dahlia said. "Our bride and groom have crafted vows for one another." She gestured to Grace, who blinked rapidly to hold back her tears.

"Dearest Holden," she began, squeezing his hands, "you are one of the kindest, most thoughtful men I have ever known. I am honored to have found someone who so deeply treasures me, and I will spend the rest of my days doing my best to show you how much you mean to me. You are my best friend, the other half of my heart, and I consider it my greatest joy to share a life with you. I promise to love you and you alone for all the rest of my days, to share in your dreams, in your victories and losses, your happiness and pain. I take you as my husband, the other half of my heart, the other piece of my soul."

"Grace," Holden breathed, reaching up to clasp her face in his hands. "You are more than I ever dared dream for. Your pure heart and deep love inspire me. You choosing me is the fulfillment of all my greatest hopes. My heart, my future, and my strength are yours. I vow to cherish you, protect you, and to be faithful to you all of my days. I will fight for you to have the best life, to never want for anything, and I will stand by your side to support your in all your dreams. There is and never will be anyone else."

Dahlia smirked. "In recognition of the vows you have made, seal them with a kiss." She winked.

Holden wrapped his arms about Grace's waist, dipping her low as he claimed her mouth.

Mother, Cordelia, Fitz, my sisters, and I cheered and applauded.

As we trudged back toward the castle, Fitz intertwined our fingers and pulled me close to his side. "That reminded me of our wedding day."

I laughed softly. "That was nothing like ours."

But Fitz shook his head, wrapping his arm around me and tucking me into his side. "I remember your spirit captivating me. I might not have shown it, and I may have tried to resist it, but I know now I was utterly smitten, even then." He leaned in, his lips brushing my ear. "And how could I not be?" he murmured. "You are my perfect match in every way. You have made me a better man, and I am forever thankful for that. For you."

Left speechless, I stopped in the snow, turning in his arms to wrap him in an embrace. "I love you," I whispered.

Stomping past us, Lina rolled her eyes, though her grin betrayed her. "Such sentimentality."

Fitz chuckled as he took my head and we started walking again, following our family and friends back toward the castle. "How could I not be consumed with emotion by my queen?"

My heart jolted against my rib cage at the reminder of what was to come.

The next morning, Lina helped me into a rich blue dress adorned with silver beads and lace formed to mimic a dazzling night sky. She left my hair unbound, spilling in a loose curtain over my shoulders. Then I slipped into a pair of boots and tucked my dagger into a thigh sheath. When I was ready, I stepped into the hall to find Fitz already waiting for me, having returned from whatever business once again took him away earlier.

"Holden and Cordelia will join us outside the throne room," Fitz said in a low voice.

Heart thundering in my ears, I nodded, taking his hand in mine and letting his warm, calloused fingers comfort me. We strolled through the halls and down the stairs, a company of guards falling into step behind us along the way.

Outside the throne room, Cordelia and Holden already waited for us, both dressed in formal attire in shades of deepest blue and silver. Cordelia flashed me a reassuring smile and Fitz squeezed my hand.

Then the guards shoved open the doors and we all burst inside at once.

Across the room, two ebony thrones awaited Fitz and me.

Every courtier in the room watched the royal siblings and me with varied expressions of awe, respect, fear, hatred, or anger. My eyes lingered on those that looked the most upset with the shift in rule, taking mental note of those that might cause the most trouble or try to start a resistance.

When we paused on the dais holding the thrones, it was Holden who spoke first, his words firm and unwavering. "We are here to crown our new king and queen."

My husband's demeanor was chillingly cool, reminding me of the calm before a storm. He was prepared for anything, and he was going to demand obedience and respect from his court. "It is time to choose your allegiance. It is time to pledge your loyalty to my wife—your new queen, the one that both the land and I have chosen. My magic and the power of our kingdom flows through her. Do you vow to accept her? Will you bend your knee to show her the respect she deserves?"

Murmurs of assent arose as the nobility, servants, and guards scattered about the room all dropped to their knees.

Taking my hand, Fitz led me to my throne. "Behold your queen," he said, lifting his voice to the crowd. "She has wielded the magic of the land itself, slain the powerful hag Deidre, and called upon spirit magic to send a soul to the afterlife. Anyone who dares question her right to rule at my side as my equal will suffer our wrath, and anyone else who dares to threaten her will not see mercy."

The assemblage dipped their heads in acknowledgement, no one daring to rise.

As a servant brought forward two gleaming wooden cases, Cordelia took them from him and approached Fitz and me. "Kneel and accept the burden and honor of ruling, serving, and protecting Ashwood, its magic, and its people."

I had already taken vows when I'd accepted the crown as Princess and Fitz's wife, which meant that this ceremony was much simpler and shorter. Cordelia wasted no time in placing each silver crown upon our heads. I marveled at the intricate patterns the leaves formed, the way its surface and every perfect diamond set within it glistened in the sunlight. When it rested upon my head, its weight was a sobering reminder of the responsibilities and danger I would carry for many years to come.

Cordelia's blue eyes shone with pride and her smile was victorious as she turned away from Fitz and me and faced the room. "Rise and greet your new rulers, King Fitz Ashwood and Queen Elle Blackford!"

The entire court stood and erupted into applause and shouts.

"May your reign be long and prosperous!"

"Long live the king and queen!"

"May your wine be strong and your magic stronger!" someone shouted.

I glanced at Fitz, who grinned, pulling me close and pressing a kiss to my forehead. "I'm still afraid I'm not ready." I whispered my confession beneath the shouts around us.

"It's a mark of a great ruler to never feel ready. It means you will always be striving to learn and better yourself. You will make the best of rulers, my queen of stars and spirits."

THE END

Thank you for reading Queen of Stars and Spirits! If you have a moment, please leave an honest review on Amazon.

ACKNOWLEDGEMENTS

Thank you so much to all the readers who fell in love with Fitz and Elle and messaged me about it. Thanks for your passion and your excitement. You inspired me to write this novella, and it was such a comfort. During this wild year, diving back into this world was so very needed. I hope you enjoy this story as much as I enjoyed writing it.

Thanks to Sheree and Malcolm for encouraging me along the way. But also distracting me with texts, cat jokes, and word puzzles. Naturally.

And of course, thank you to my alpha/critical readers: Beth, Brittany, Natalia, Sheree, and Tricia. As always, you made this story so much better.

ABOUT THE AUTHOR

Rachel L. Schade was born on the first day of summer in a small town in Michigan. She attended The Ohio State University to learn how to write obnoxiously long papers, cite people who use big words, and discuss her passion: books. She has a great love for the color blue, sunshine, chocolate, and not folding her laundry. Currently she lives in Ohio with her husband, daughter, and fur babies, and surrounds herself with books and coffee on a regular basis.

www.rachelschadeauthor.com

www.ingramcontent.com/pod-product-compliance
Lightning Source LLC
Chambersburg PA
CBHW021924170626
46807CB00007B/2979